"What did you expect?" Isla asked softly.

"You left, and *Daadi* forbid me to see you again." Her father, a minister and very strict, had insisted that she walk the path of obedience. As much as she wanted it to, love alone couldn't bridge the divide between Amish and *Englisch*. The two might coexist, but the lines ran parallel.

And never the twain shall meet.

Evan cleared his throat. "I was genuinely happy for you both. It's what folks are supposed to do, you know? Get married, have a family..."

"*Ja.* We did."

Overwhelmed by the emotions gripping her heart, Isla returned to her cooking. The pain in her chest grew stronger, a reminder that some wounds never truly healed, and that some choices left scars that time could never erase. Sixteen years ago, the urge to follow Evan into the *Englisch* world was a temptation she'd found hard to resist. She'd never admit it, but she'd considered defying her *vater's* command.

She'd let the only man she'd ever loved go...and had regretted it ever since.

Pamela Desmond Wright grew up in a small, dusty Texas town. Like the Amish, Pamela is a fan of the simple life. Her childhood includes memories of the olden days: old-fashioned oil lamps, cooking over an authentic wood-burning stove and making popcorn over a crackling fire at her grandparents' cabin. The authentic log cabin Pamela grew up playing in was donated to the Muleshoe Heritage Center in Muleshoe, Texas, where it is on public display.

Books by Pamela Desmond Wright

Love Inspired

Visit the Author Profile page at LoveInspired.com.

AN AMISH WIDOW'S HOPE

PAMELA DESMOND WRIGHT

LOVE INSPIRED
INSPIRATIONAL ROMANCE

LOVE INSPIRED®

INSPIRATIONAL ROMANCE

ISBN-13: 978-1-335-23038-6

Recycling programs
for this product may
not exist in your area.

An Amish Widow's Hope

Love Inspired
22 Adelaide St. West, 41st Floor
Toronto, Ontario M5H 4E3, Canada
www.LoveInspired.com

HarperCollins Publishers
Macken House, 39/40 Mayor Street Upper,
Dublin 1, D01 C9W8, Ireland
www.HarperCollins.com

Printed in U.S.A.

Fear thou not; for I am with thee: be not dismayed;
for I am thy God: I will strengthen thee;
yea, I will help thee; yea, I will uphold thee
with the right hand of my righteousness.
—*Isaiah* 41:10

To my big sissie, Jeri Patterson. For your love and support—I'm so grateful for you.

A special thank-you also goes to my editor, Melissa Endlich—your keen insights and steady guidance make each book stronger. And to my amazing agent, Tamela Hancock Murray—your unwavering belief in me and my stories is a gift I treasure.

...and to Carl Marino, who inspired Sheriff Miller.

Chapter One

❧

"Unit 1, come in. Unit 1, Sheriff Miller, do you copy?"

Eyes bleary with exhaustion, Evan Miller reached for the mike. "Go ahead, Dispatch," he said, his voice gravelly. Ten hours into an eight-hour shift, and he was utterly frazzled.

The dispatcher's voice crackled over the airwaves. "We've got another break-in."

Evan winced as more details emerged. Once again, the culprit had struck in an Amish neighborhood.

"Copy that, Dispatch. I'm on it."

"Ten-four," the radio crackled back.

Flipping on his lights, he left the siren off—no need to scare the already shaken townsfolk. Making a quick U-turn, he sped toward the destination, keeping an eye out for anyone or anything that looked out of place.

Vital minutes ticked by.

Turning down an avenue paved with cobblestones, he passed cozy houses, weathered barns and bountiful gardens. Nestled within the historic district of Burr Oak and zoned to allow for the keeping of horses and other livestock, the location was primarily inhabited by Plain folks. Stately oak trees lined the street, their thick branches forming a verdant canopy. Each home stood as a testament to the skills and labor of its inhabitants. Wide porches beckoned visitors to sit awhile, and the scent of homemade bread often mingled with the fresh, earthy aroma of tilled soil.

Here, life and business intertwined seamlessly. Hand-painted signs adorned the edges of several properties, advertising the available diverse goods and wares crafted by skilled hands. Simple folks, the Amish worked hard to provide an honest living for their families.

He searched for the address that dispatch had relayed. Finally, a neat home perched on a large lot came into view, set behind a picket fence. Blue shutters provided a cheery contrast against whitewashed walls. The trim lawn and flower beds reflected the owner's love for gardening. Potted plants enhanced the inviting entrance. A sign leaning against a sawhorse read Plain & Simple Sewing.

After parking at the curb, he headed through the gate. The late spring afternoon was blustery and dark clouds gathered, thick with the promise of a storm. Holding his clipboard tightly so the wind couldn't snatch his paperwork away, he strode up the walkway.

Drawn by his cruiser, curious onlookers peered out their windows. The Amish tolerated *Englisch* law enforcement, but that didn't mean they embraced it. Still, folks were spooked by the break-ins. And rightfully so. This latest string of thefts was something more malicious than the usual petty larcenies. The culprit was going after people who wouldn't fight back.

The front door swung open before he stepped onto the porch. A middle-aged woman of stout build stared down at him.

"About time you got here, Sheriff." Face red with frustration, she clutched a long wooden spoon. "Nice of you to dawdle as if there were no urgency. Abner called 911 twenty minutes ago."

Oh, no. His last encounter with Verna Pilcher had left a bitter taste in his mouth. Leader of the community watch, she was his fiercest critic. No matter what he did, it always fell short of her expectations. She believed he should be on duty every hour of every day.

"I got here as soon as I could." Overworked and understaffed, the department was barely managing to keep up with the surge in crime. "You want to hold the judgment and tell me what happened?"

"What happened?" Verna echoed, cheeks flushing a deeper shade of purple. "Some no-good thief breezed right in. That's what happened."

"And I'll do all I can to catch him," he said and gestured toward the entrance. "If you don't mind, I'll need to go inside."

Huffing, Verna stepped aside. "Hardworking folks shouldn't have to live in fear in their own homes," she complained. "Something has to be done."

"I hear you, and I'm doing everything in my power to put a stop to it." He tipped his hat with a nod. "Now, if you'll excuse me, I've got work to do."

Passing her by, he went inside. The interior of the home was simple but immaculate. Arranged for the reception of customers, a small parlor harbored an old-fashioned treadle sewing machine, its cast-iron frame polished to a gleaming shine. Dressmakers' dummies stood nearby, adorned with garments in various stages of completion. Each piece told a story of meticulous care and dedication to the craft of sewing. A large bay window adorned with lace curtains added a touch of charm. Unfortunately, remnants of the crime were also evident. Drawers had been rifled through and other small items overturned. A silent witness to greed, an empty cashbox lay discarded on the floor.

A woman and two children sat on a nearby love seat. The siblings clung to each other. The girl, slightly older, tried to appear brave, but her trembling body betrayed her unease.

"Is everyone all right?"

"*Ja.* I think so." Dabbing teary eyes, the woman lowered her handkerchief.

"Can you—" he started to ask, but the rest never materialized. He couldn't help but stare at her. Slender and fine-boned, her crystal blue gaze was strikingly familiar. Clad in a widow's weeds, her hair was pinned beneath a black *kapp*. A few long strands had escaped, framing her face with wispy blonde curls.

He blinked, taken aback. Pulse missing a beat, recognition kicked in. *Isla Stohl*… The girl he'd known was now a woman, and the sight of her took his breath away. Every feature, from the delicate arch of her eyebrows to the curve of her lips, was perfectly sculpted. Images of their shared childhood flooded his mind; the laughter, the secrets, the innocent delight of *Rumspringa* as they explored the *Englisch* world together, tasting the forbidden freedom that lay beyond their community. He could almost feel the electric thrill of their first kiss, a moment charged with promise and passion.

"I didn't realize…"

Isla tilted her head thoughtfully. "It has been quite some time, hasn't it?"

"Yes, it has." He hadn't expected to come face-to-face with his past when he'd walked through the door. Seeing her again rattled him—quick, unexpected and hard to shake off.

More uninvited images surged back. The joy of their courtship was soon overshadowed by the sorrow of their breakup. He remembered the agony of his decision to leave the Amish, torn between the expectations of his family and his ambition to be more than a simple pig farmer. In the end, he'd chosen to depart. But standing before her now, he questioned if he'd truly understood what he was leaving behind when he walked away from that life. And from her.

"Not the way I'd imagined seeing you again," she said, a mixture of sadness and something deeper reflected in her gaze.

Evan pulled himself back to the present, donning his professional demeanor like armor. The past was a bridge long crossed. Today, he had a job to do.

"Yeah. Not exactly my choice either."

"I suppose we'll have to make the best of it," she allowed. "Please, do what you must."

Snagging a pen, he lifted his clipboard. "Were you home when the incident occurred?"

"I was not." Pausing for a breath, she explained, "I'd taken a break to fetch the *kinder* from the park. I'd barely unlocked the door before I caught a glimpse of a man dashing through the *haus*." Pointing, she added, "He went through there."

Following the directions, Evan walked into the kitchen. The back door stood ajar, the frame splintered and warped from the violent intrusion.

Hanging off-kilter on its hinges, it creaked ominously with every faint draft. Fragments from its glass face lay scattered on the floor.

As always, the culprit had made a clean getaway. He'd had no one to chase him or hold him accountable. Evan was the one who had to look the victims in the eye and promise things would get better.

He returned to the parlor. "Did you get a look at the perp?"

Discomfort flickered in her expression. "I only caught a glimpse, but he was dressed in Amish clothing."

"Did anyone see his face? Or any other features you might recognize?"

The witnesses all shook their heads.

"He was going out as we were coming in. A few minutes earlier, and we'd have walked right in on him."

"Be thankful you didn't," Verna Pilcher declared. "Why, there's no telling what could have happened."

Isla drew a steadying breath. "*Gott* had a hand over us."

"*Daed's* keeping an eye from heaven, too," Joel said.

"He is, *sohn*," she said, laying a hand on the youngster's arm. "He always has, and he always will."

Emotion tightened Evan's throat. He knew Isla's

name wasn't Stohl anymore. It was Bruhn. After they'd broken up, she'd gone on to marry his best friend.

"My condolences on your loss."

"We miss him," she said, declining to say more.

An uncomfortable silence stepped between them. Unspoken words and unresolved feelings created a palpable tension neither seemed ready to break.

Evan didn't judge her reluctance to share personal details. They hadn't spoken in years, at least a decade or more. Nor had he attended Owen's funeral. What right did he have to mourn alongside them when he'd chosen to reject his heritage?

Embarrassed, he tapped his pen against his clipboard. The sooner he gathered the facts, the sooner he could leave. "I take it you kept cash on hand?" Kneeling by the cashbox, he made a note to have it dusted for prints. Just in case.

"*Ja*," she said.

"How much?"

"Everything."

"How much is everything?"

"Two thousand." She pointed toward a large rolltop desk. "Owen always kept our money locked in the drawer." Irony twisted her lips. "It's always been safe."

Rising, he walked over to examine the damage. Several drawers had been pried open, probably with the same tool used to jimmy the back door.

Though some Amish were fine with the safekeep-
ing a bank offered, others preferred to keep their
money in hand. Most Plain folks also didn't have
any security in place, either. It would be easy for
someone to look around and figure things out.

"Did he take anything else?"

"He took my pocketknife, the one *Daed* gave
me for my birthday," Joel blurted, and his lower
lip trembled.

"My piggy bank was smashed, too," her daughter whispered, voice barely audible. "All my pin
money is gone."

The news didn't sit well with Evan. *He's getting bolder.* The fact that the intruder was enter-
ing personal spaces bothered him.

"If there's anything else, be sure and let me
know."

Verna Pilcher stepped in. "What for?" she
squawked. "All you've done so far is a whole lot
of nothing!" She waved her spoon so vigorously
that it was in danger of taking flight.

"Cut me a little slack," he said, exasperation
creeping into his tone. "Please. I'm doing the best
I can."

Verna eyed him. "Sure you are, Sheriff."

Stung by her sarcasm, Evan's hand rose to his
temple. Operating on caffeine and adrenaline, a
stress headache had plagued him for days. By
failing to catch the unknown suspect, he'd let the
citizens down. He couldn't stand the idea of in-

nocent people living in fear. No one deserved to have their homes invaded or their livelihoods threatened.

Certainly not his former best friend's widow.

He sneaked a glance toward Isla. Huddled on the sofa, her arms were wrapped protectively around her children. Her eyes, wide and haunted, mirrored a deep well of grief.

A jolt of protectiveness surged through him. More tangible than the badge he carried, the burden of duty pressed heavily on his shoulders. This wasn't just another case. Isla was a woman devastated not once, but twice, by cruel fate.

With a resolute breath, he made a silent vow. Though he couldn't turn back time or erase what had happened, he could ease her anxiety by standing as a barrier against the chaos threatening to engulf her.

Isla's hands trembled as she swept up the glass littering her kitchen floor. The invasion of her home was frightening, leaving her with nothing but an overwhelming sense of loss. Acting with ruthless disregard, the thief had worked hard to pry open her back door.

Blinking back tears, she pushed the remnants of glass into a dustpan. The damage was devastating. Her *vater* had crafted the door from rich, golden oak as a gift for her wedding. Planed and sanded to a silken finish, the door's true marvel was its stained-glass face. Built for each entrance of the house, the twin set symbolized the love and devotion he wished for his daughter's new home.

Now her father's labor of love was in pieces. Gideon Stohl had later died from an accident in his workshop. While the frame could be rebuilt, the original door was ruined. All that remained was its lone mate. The pair would never stand together again.

Dumping the shards into a nearby trash pail, she wiped her hands on her apron. The kitchen looked better cleaned up. She studied the empty chair at the head of the table. Eleven months ago, the center of her world had been ripped away. Diagnosed at stage four, Owen's cancer had been discovered too late to attempt treatment. He'd died within weeks of learning his nagging cough was something much worse. His laughter, his steady presence—all were gone, leaving behind a void that filled every corner of the small home.

A lump rose in her throat. *I don't know how much more I can take.*

She'd done her best to hold things together. A cobbler by trade, Owen had never made a lot of money. But combined with her sewing shop, they'd had enough to comfortably raise their *youngies*. On her own, she was struggling. Each day was a battle to balance the cost of fabric and supplies with the need to feed and clothe her children. Since Owen's passing, the world seemed frayed, her life unraveling no matter how hard she tried to hold it all together.

The weight of loss pressed down on her, a quiet desperation settling as the walls seemed to close in. Every cent she'd saved was gone. She had no one to turn to, no close *familie* left to lean on. Owen's parents, though kind, were burdened by their own struggles. After her *daed* passed, her *mamm* had remarried and followed her new husband to an Amish settlement in Maine. Her siblings, too, were busy building their own lives, distant both in miles and heart.

Overwhelmed, she bowed her head. "You're going to have to handle this, Lord," she murmured. "I can't do this myself." Her plea was simple but heartfelt. Prayer was the oxygen sustaining her spirit. Whenever she felt engulfed by darkness, *Gott* illuminated her path. In these small moments of communion, she found the strength to carry on.

The sound of heavy footsteps interrupted her thoughts.

"Hey," a familiar voice said. "Everything okay?"

Isla turned to see Evan Miller standing in the doorway. "Fine," she replied, her tone going sharp.

He didn't flinch. "We're almost done. Another ten minutes should wrap it up and we'll go."

"I hope so." What else could she say? Since his arrival, he'd done everything he'd said he would.

As promised, another deputy had arrived to help process the evidence. After photographing the damage, the two men had also brushed for prints. Watching him work had impressed her. His commitment spoke volumes.

Both officers had done their best to answer questions, attempting to calm shaken residents.

"We've made progress," he said. "Deputy Lopez located a crowbar under the hedge, probably the one used to break in. He also found a fake beard. Since you said the suspect was dressed in Amish-style clothes, I'm going to guess he's using the disguise to hide in plain sight, if you will."

"That would make sense." An Amish man carrying tools wouldn't arouse anyone's suspicions. The neighborhood was full of craftsmen hauling the equipment of their trade. No wonder the police were having trouble catching up with him. The thief blended in with the very people he robbed.

"It's doubtful we'll find prints. But we're sending them to the lab anyway. We might get a print or other DNA from touch transfer."

Nodding, Isla crossed her arms protectively over her chest. "Sounds *gut*."

"Lopez is doing a walkthrough of the house now," he continued. "Just to make sure we didn't miss anything." Now that the investigation was ending, he rubbed his eyes, visibly trying to shake off exhaustion.

Sympathy unexpectedly tugged at her heart.

Evan might have made some bad judgment calls, but there was no reason to keep punishing him for something he'd done in his youth. Time had passed, she'd matured, and life had gone on. As was expected, she'd become a *fraa*, and then a *mutter*. He was just someone she used to know. Why keep beating him up over their breakup?

"Would you like some *kaffee*? You look like you could use it."

Hand dropping, he managed a grateful smile. "That would be nice. *Danke*."

"You still speak *Deitsch*?"

"I'm rusty, but I can make myself understood. Some older Amish folks, like my *daed*, won't speak English if they don't have to."

"He still doesn't," she said.

"Some things never change." Another shrug followed. "Doesn't matter, I guess. Far as he's concerned, I died years ago."

Isla remembered that, too. After Evan took a job that required him to be armed, his *daed*'s demeanor had turned icy. Staunch traditionalists like Jonah Miller felt leaving the community was a stain on the family's honor, but to carry a weapon as well was more than he could bear. It wasn't a shunning, but it was close. Evan's name was taboo in the Miller home, and he was not allowed to visit his *mamm* or siblings. Currently, he could engage with the community. A few even welcomed having someone in law enforcement who understood the ways of Plain folks. But he was always kept at a distance, like any *Englisch* outsider.

Unsure what to say, she busied herself filling the percolator. She'd just set it on the stove to heat when Deputy Lopez entered with Joel and Olivia. The children's faces were pale.

"I've gone through every room," Lopez reported. "Nothing else seems to be missing."

Shaken by the invasion, Isla felt like the ground was disintegrating beneath her feet. "I understand him taking my money, but how could he steal from *youngies*?"

"Because he can," Evan answered simply. "It's his way of proving he's in control."

"He's gotten away so far, so why not try for more?" Deputy Lopez added.

"Which is why we need to get that evidence processed as soon as possible," Evan prodded.

"I'm on it," Lopez said, already turning away. With everything he needed in hand, the deputy quickly exited.

Forgotten atop the stove, the percolator boiled over. Hot liquid frothed up the spout, creating a miniature waterfall that cascaded down the sides.

Startled by the commotion, Isla rushed over, wielding a kitchen towel to stem the flow. With deft hands, she removed the metal pot from the heat, its lid clattering as it came to rest on the counter.

Nerves frayed, tears blurred her vision. This simple mishap was the last straw on an already burdened back. She couldn't help but feel a deep sense of vulnerability. The safety she'd taken for granted in her Amish neighborhood seemed fragile and fleeting.

The squall outside suddenly rocked the damaged door. Leaves and other debris tumbled across the floor, driven in by a gust of wind. Lightning flashed, followed by the booming roll of thunder. Another blustery spring tempest was on the way.

"That's a problem." Passing her by, Evan pushed the door shut. With the frame, lock and window shattered, there was no way to secure it. "I think you should find somewhere else to stay until this is repaired."

Looking between the stove and the door, Isla slowly shook her head. The *haus* was her sanctuary, the place where every corner held a memory. Carried across the threshold as a young bride, she'd raised both her *kinder* within the shelter of its walls.

"*Nein*. This is my home, and I won't be driven out by thieves."

"You've got no protection here," Evan insisted, pressing harder. "We could probably do something to block it off temporarily, but it won't hold long. Are you sure you couldn't stay with a neighbor until repairs are made?"

"When it is fixed, can you promise we'll be safe?"

Her question caught him off guard, and he met her gaze with uncertainty. "You know I can't."

Isla planted her hands on her hips. No one was going to scare her away from her home. No one. The notion of borrowing lumber and nailing the door shut herself flitted through her mind. Anything to make the whole horrible day go away.

"Then why bother? It's not like I can just pack up and go, anyway. The children have pets, school… And I have work, commissions to deliver if I expect to bring in an income."

He didn't blink twice. "I understand the inconvenience. But I think you should leave for a few days. If nothing else, it would give us a chance to try and catch up with the perp."

"You haven't yet," she pointed out, echoing Verna's complaint.

Listening to the adults going back and forth, Olivia folded her arms across her chest. "*Mamm*, I'm scared…"

Joel edged closer to his sister. Barely nine, his small frame trembled. "What if that man comes back?"

A fresh rise of nausea tightened Isla's insides as she absorbed the seriousness of the situation. Her home, usually a sanctuary of peace and order, felt foreign and threatening. She could still hear the echo of the intruder's heavy footsteps as he'd exited the house.

She blinked, trying to hide the tears that threatened to spill over. The last thing she wanted was for Evan Miller to see her weakness, especially now.

"I just…can't…" She had no money to rent a room, and no relatives close by. Nor would it feel right to pile in on a neighbor on short notice.

Concern deepening, Evan frowned. His gaze traveled over the broken door, then back to her face, searching for a way to bridge the gap that years of silence had carved.

"Then I guess I should get this taken care of."

"It's not your responsibility."

The lawman's steely expression softened, but his voice remained firm. "It is," he pronounced with an air of finality. "If that guy thinks you can recognize him, he might decide to come back. I can't afford to take any chances. Better safe than sorry."

Chapter Two

As a married woman, Isla had learned a fundamental truth about men: when they set their minds to do something, they followed through with unwavering determination. Over the years, she had also learned the wisdom of stepping back and allowing them to proceed without interference.

Evan was no exception. He'd promised to take care of things, and he did exactly that, demonstrating the same resolute commitment. It didn't matter that she couldn't offer a single cent in payment, nor that the task would consume the better part of his time that day. His focus was on helping, and he set about the work with quiet diligence.

After taking a few measurements, the sheriff had briefly disappeared. A half hour later, he'd returned from the hardware store with everything needed to make the repairs. Catching sight of the lawman as he'd attempted to wrestle the new door out of the back of his cruiser, Abner Pilcher had also offered help. Lugging over a heavy toolbox, the old man had set to rebuilding the frame with practiced ease.

And then it was done.

"I think that will do it," Evan said, testing the new deadbolt.

Abner offered his approval, his weathered face framed by a graying beard. "I think we did a *gut* job," he said, making a last inspection. The new door fit snugly in the frame, sturdy and solid. The heavy-duty lock kept it securely in place.

Grateful to have a solid barrier between herself and the outside world, Isla looked between the two men. "It looks fine. I'm thankful to have it."

As the men had worked, she'd felt a surge of gratitude. The cop and the carpenter were like two sides of a coin—one representing the modern world's laws and protections, the other embodying the community's willingness to lend a hand to those in need. Though the sense of violation from being robbed still lingered heavily in her heart, watching them instilled a sense of hope. It wasn't just about fixing the damage; it was about restoring a semblance of security and normalcy to her disrupted life. Somehow this simple act of kindness made the day a little better. It was a reminder that even in the wake of misfortune, there were still decent folks who would come to the aid of others.

Evan handed over the screwdriver he'd borrowed. "Thank you for the help."

"Despite what Verna says, I know you're doing your best, Sheriff."

"Somehow this fellow is always one step ahead," Evan admitted, shaking his head. "At least I have an idea how he's getting away with it."

"I pray you catch him soon," Abner said, giving the door one final inspection. "The man's got a wicked heart for sure if he'd steal from a widow."

Looking at the newly mended door, the lawman's jaw hardened. "I have to agree."

Abner glanced toward the window, taking note of the worsening storm. Outside, the lightning flashed harder and faster, followed by rolling booms of thunder. "Suppose I'd better get going." Gathering his tools, he prepared to depart. "It'll take a lot of trouble to get that thing open now," he commented to Isla. "You can sleep easier tonight."

"The entry sensor will let you know the minute it comes open," Evan added.

Isla eyed the battery-powered alarm he'd insisted on installing. "I hope I can learn that thing. I'd hate to set it off when there wasn't an emergency."

"I'll show you how to program it before I leave," he said, brushing sawdust off his uniform.

Abner hefted his toolbox. "Guess I'd better get on home. Verna's making her chicken noodle casserole." Grimacing a little, he added, "Unfortunately."

Isla smiled in sympathy. An enthusiastic cook, Verna Pilcher wasn't a competent one. The dishes she'd carried over after Owen's death were downright inedible. Still, she'd thanked Verna for her generosity before quietly discarding the food.

"Would a batch of cookies make it better?"

"I could stand some." Thin as a rail, Abner never turned down any home-baked treats.

"How about chocolate chip, with lots of extra pecans?"

"Looking forward to it." Toolbox in hand, he prepared to depart.

Isla escorted the old man to the front steps. "Thank you for all you've done."

Before stepping outside, Abner turned to face her. "Just remember, *Gott* will see you through this dark time. And Verna and I are right down the street if you need anything."

"*Danke.*"

The old man smiled. "Be strong, child. And lock that door tight." Giving a final nod, he stepped outside, his figure bent against the gusts of wind.

Lightning slashed through the sky then, illuminating the street in a ghostly white veil for a split second before plunging it back into shadows. The thunder that followed was a deafening roar, shaking the ground beneath her feet. Thick clouds swirled. And then the rain came. Hard.

Isla's breath caught. The day that had begun

with sunshine and promise had turned into a cold, miserable night.

"Ah, springtime in Texas," a voice drawled from behind.

Feeling the sudden drop in the temperature, Isla shivered. "Hope it doesn't throw off any tornadoes."

"That time of year," he acknowledged. "I just hope the electric holds. Folks always call when the lights go out."

"Must be *Englischer*s." Not a single *haus* in the older neighborhoods was wired for electricity. Most Amish preferred to light their homes with more traditional methods. Some had turned to solar panels, as the *Ordnung* allowed the use of *Gott*'s natural resources. As Owen had preferred kerosene, she kept a few old-timey lamps in the parlor. But now these were only for display and not actual use. For safety's sake, she preferred battery-powered lamps. Flammable liquids were best kept out of the reach of *youngies* and pets.

"*Ja*, *Englischer*s," he confirmed with a laugh. "Some folks can't handle the dark. However, I do wonder what they think we can do about the issue. It's not like we're the ones who fix the power lines."

Isla tilted her head thoughtfully. "Perhaps they believe the law should be able to handle anything, even the weather."

Evan laughed, a rich, genuine sound that cut

through the storm's din. "I reckon they're sorely disappointed when they learn just how little control we have over things."

"I suppose we have to learn some things are simply in *Gott*'s hands," she said. "All we can do is pray and try to get through the difficulties."

"Pretty much." Evan leaned forward, scanning the sky. "Guess I'll make a run for it since this storm isn't going to ease up anytime soon."

Isla hesitated. The cost of the supplies had come out of his pocket. When she'd protested, explaining that she couldn't afford to pay him back right away, he'd waved her concerns aside.

Despite his reassurances, she couldn't help but feel a pang of guilt. His generosity had been unexpected, and she worried about the burden he'd taken on for her sake. The thought of being indebted to him, even if he insisted it was of no consequence, gnawed at her.

"You haven't had anything all afternoon," she said. "You're welcome to join us for supper."

Evan hesitated, his gaze flicking to the floor before meeting hers again. "I don't want to impose." The wariness in his voice betrayed more than simple politeness.

"You wouldn't be," she countered, more insistent this time.

He exhaled, almost a sigh, then nodded once. "All right. Thanks. That would be great."

"*Gut.*" Moving with purpose, she crossed back

into the kitchen. The night's meal of potato and ham hock soup wasn't fancy, but it would be filling.

Evan followed. "Anything I can do?"

Isla lifted the percolator, filling a cup with fresh *kaffee*. Remaking it after the earlier disaster, she'd managed not to scald the brew. "Try not to get in the way."

Kaffee served, she opened the refrigerator. Moving a large pot to the stovetop, she adjusted the flame, ensuring it wouldn't heat too quickly and ruin the flavors that had melded together overnight. "The soup is leftover, but I'll make fresh corn bread." Normally, Olivia and Joel would help with supper, but her concern for their safety had prompted her to keep them out of the way as the men worked to make the repairs.

"Sounds good," he said.

First gathering the ingredients from the pantry, Isla placed a stoneware mixing bowl on the counter. With practiced hands, she combined everything smoothly and then slid the pan into the oven. "It won't take long to bake."

He eyed the propane stove. "Looks like you and Owen moved into modern times."

Heart swelling with emotion, Isla glanced over her shiny stainless-steel appliances. Her late husband had always been a frugal man, saving every penny to ensure a stable future for their family.

"Owen had the kitchen updated to propane a

few years ago," she explained, running her fingers over the smooth laminate countertop. Knowing how much she'd struggled with the old wood-fired stove, he'd arranged the new stove as a surprise for her birthday. Her *ehemann*'s love for her was evident in every detail. He'd thought of everything, ensuring she could manage the household chores with ease. This stove heated quickly, allowing her to cook meals in half the time. The refrigerator kept valuable food fresh for longer periods, reducing wastage. And the water heater provided hot water on demand, a luxury she'd never experienced before.

"He was a good guy," Evan said, his voice tinged with nostalgia. "I liked him, a lot. When I heard that he was going to marry you..."

Sensing the catch in his voice, Isla gazed back. In that instant, Evan was no longer a man who'd confidently walked away from his past. He was a boy again, standing on the edge of adulthood, faced with the daunting prospect of choices that would shape the rest of his life. The years of separation, the life choices, the different worlds they now inhabited melted away, leaving just the two of them, suspended in a moment of raw, poignant connection.

Pushing aside the past, she allowed herself to see him again in the present, no longer a feckless youth. Time had added not only muscle but maturity. Standing well over six feet, his lanky frame was a deceptive veil for the strength coiled in his sinewy frame. Strands of silver threaded his temples, whispering of the wisdom and experience earned.

A knot formed in her throat as a mix of emotions swirled: Aching sorrow for what could have been. Pride in seeing him excel in his chosen role. A sentimental longing for the innocence of their youth.

"What did you expect?" she asked. "You left, and *Daadi* forbade me to see you again." Her father, a very strict minister, had insisted that she walk the path of obedience. As much as she wanted it to, love alone couldn't bridge the divide between Amish and *Englischer*s. The two might coexist, but the lines ran parallel.

And never the twain shall meet, she reminded herself.

Scrubbing a hand across his mouth, Evan cleared his throat. "I was genuinely happy for you both. It's what folks are supposed to do, you know? Get married, have a family…"

"*Ja*. We did."

Overwhelmed by the emotions gripping her heart, Isla returned to her cooking. The pain in her chest grew stronger, a reminder that some wounds never truly healed, and that some choices left scars that time could never erase. Sixteen years ago, the urge to follow Evan had been a temptation she'd found hard to resist. She'd never admit it, but she'd considered defying her *vater*'s command. Fear of the unknown and *Gott*'s judgment toward the disobedient had held her back.

She'd come to love Owen in time, gently and honestly. But it was Evan Miller who had always quietly held her heart. Losing him was a regret she'd always carried.

Reaching a crossroads in his life, Evan had left the Amish. He'd also walked away from Isla. A few months later, Owen Bruhn had stepped in and married her.

Occasionally, Evan had glimpsed the couple shopping at the farmers' market or attending an auction or other charity event held to support church members. A nod of recognition, a few brief remarks. Those had been the extent of their interactions. Like most Plain folks, they preferred to socialize among their own. *Englischer*s were tolerated, but that was all.

You're not one of them anymore, he reminded himself. Regrets? Yes, he had many. Too many to count. But wondering how his life might have turned out if he'd made different choices would do no good.

Still, the weight of what might have been lingered. But seeing Isla today was a walk down memory lane, nothing more. Inviting him for a meal was her way of being kind. No doubt she felt obligated.

Shaking off his thoughts, he forced himself back into the present. With the storm raging outside, the kitchen was a haven of warmth and comfort. The air thickened with the scent of onions, potatoes and herbs. Corn bread baked in the oven.

"That smells pretty good."

"There's not much meat, but it will fill the belly."

"How are you doing since Owen passed?"

"I'm holding my own." Unease flickering across her face, Isla quickly turned away, giving the soup an anxious stir.

Having learned to read body language, Evan recognized the telltale signs of stress. He hadn't failed to miss the slight furrow in her brow or the frown tugging at the edges of her mouth. Even though most Amish were self-sufficient, their way of life still required money for essential items and services that they could not produce or trade for among themselves. Necessities like propane required the need for cash. Not content with completely wiping out Isla's savings, the perpetrator had even resorted to stealing from a child.

Her remark prodded at him. He couldn't just stand by and watch her struggle. "How about I offer you a loan? Just until you get back on your feet."

Isla's shoulders visibly stiffened. "Thank you, but I can't accept your charity. I'll find a way to manage."

"It isn't charity. You can pay me back whenever you're able."

Snapping off the fire beneath the pot, she turned. "That's a generous offer. But I'll manage on my own. I do have commissions, and once they're complete, I'll be paid."

He sighed. She'd always had a stubborn streak and once she set her mind, it rarely changed. "All right. But if you need it, it's there."

"You've already done more than enough, and I can't keep taking from you. It's not your responsibility to look after me or my *kinder.*"

"It is my responsibility to make sure folks are safe." He'd pledged an oath to shield the vulnerable from harm's way and was determined to uphold it.

"And you have. Repairing my door was enough, *danke.*" Giving the soup a final stir, she checked her baking. "Ah, done." As she pulled the pan from the oven, a delightful aroma filled the kitchen, announcing the corn bread's golden-brown perfection. "I hope you're hungry," she added, flitting around to set the table with dishes and cutlery. "There's plenty."

Evan's stomach rumbled. "Anything you care to serve sounds good to me." He made a mental note to stay out of her way. He'd already crossed a line, and he didn't want to risk offending her again.

I'll have a bite and go.

After that, it was unlikely they would cross paths again anytime soon. He could always rely on Deputy Lopez to follow up on case updates. His shared history with Isla, marked by layers of unresolved tensions and unspoken truths, dictated a cautious approach. These strategies would probably be the best way to handle things.

Stepping out of the fragrant confines of the kitchen, Isla summoned the children with a gentle call that carried through the house. "Supper is ready!"

The sound of feet on wooden steps heralded their arrival. The break-in and the subsequent theft of their personal belongings had left them unsettled, their innocence marred by a brush with harsh reality. Each step toward the table seemed to carry the memories of their shared experience, a collective understanding of vulnerability and loss etched into their features.

"Take your places," Isla instructed.

Olivia, the older child, obediently hurried over. The youngest, Joel, lagged.

"Are you eating with us?" the boy asked, eyes wide with curiosity as they darted over his uniform.

Evan smiled. "I was invited."

Joel's eyes settled on his utility belt. He shrank back, fear clouding his young features. "Are you going to bring that?"

Isla's gaze flicked to his side, where his holstered weapon was visible. "Sheriff Miller," she said, her voice firm, "if you don't mind, your firearm won't be allowed at my table."

Evan glanced down. The pistol's weight on his hip served as a constant reminder of the responsibility he carried. The gun symbolized the authority granted to him by the people who had voted him into office, a physical manifestation of their trust and reliance on his ability to protect and serve. But it was also a sobering reminder that he possessed not only the capacity to preserve life but also the power to end it.

"Of course," he agreed.

"You can hang it on the coatrack," Isla suggested. "It will be out of the way there."

"Then that's what I'll do." Following her direction, he unbuckled his gun belt and carefully hung it on a hook in the parlor by the door. "All good?" he asked, returning to the kitchen.

"*Ja*," Isla said, pointing to a chair at the table. "Please, sit."

With a sigh of relief, Evan took his seat, feeling the day's weariness seep into his bones. The wooden dining table, worn from years of use, stood as a sturdy centerpiece, adorned with a simple yet elegant tablecloth. The meal promised a feast for both the senses and the soul.

Isla bustled around, ladling the steaming soup into each bowl. She then placed the corn bread in the center of the table, the crispy edges promising a delightful crunch. "Would you like buttermilk, or shall I refill your *kaffee*?"

Evan eyed the corn bread. Back when he was a kid, his *mamm* served corn bread and milk at almost every meal. "Buttermilk would hit the spot."

Isla poured the thick, creamy beverage into a tall glass. "Bulah Eicher brought it over just this morning. Fresh butter, too."

"Thank you," he said. "It'll be a real treat."

Taking a seat, Isla smiled at him. "As our guest, would you care to say the blessing?"

Chest tightening, Evan shook his head. The earnest boy who once believed in divine justice was now a weary man who had seen too much of the world's cruelty, questioning not just the existence of a higher power, but his own place in a seemingly godless world.

"Best leave that to those who believe," he said, hoping it was a polite way to decline without offending. "No disrespect intended."

"No need to apologize. We all have our way of getting through." She signaled her son with a gentle nod. "Joel, you're the man of the *haus* now. Would you lead us in prayer?"

Accepting the responsibility, Joel sat up straighter. "*Ja*, I will." Pressing his hands together, he closed his eyes. "*Gott*, *danke* for the food *Mamm* has made for us." He paused, his face scrunching up. "And help us not be afraid of the bad man. Please look after Sheriff Miller, um, when he's doing his hard job. Help him be strong and brave, and let him know you're always there." Small hands squeezing together a bit tighter, he pushed out the last of it. "Amen."

A lump formed in Evan's throat as he listened to the boy's simple entreaty. Each resonated with a purity that he found both comforting and humbling.

"Amen," he murmured, voice barely audible.

"That was a very nice prayer," Isla said, her voice filled with pride. She spread her napkin neatly across her lap. "Your *vater* would be proud."

Joel beamed, his young face radiant with innocence. "I tried hard."

Olivia offered a shy smile. "*Danke* for keeping us safe," she said, speaking up for the first time since they'd sat down. "It's nice to have a door again."

Isla gave him a sincere look. "Owen would thank you if he were here. Knowing your work, he always asked *Gott* to keep a hand over you."

Feeling a pang of self-consciousness, Evan shifted in his seat. Losing touch with family and friends was a bitter pill to swallow, one that had lodged itself deep. The gradual unraveling of familiar connections was a slow, relentless erosion.

"That was kind of him," he mumbled, unable to shake the feeling he was unworthy of the consideration.

The weight of his choices suddenly pressed

hard, each regret a stone in the growing pile of self-doubt. He'd turned away from the very source of comfort and guidance that had once defined his daily life.

The distance separating them grew, not just physically, but emotionally. Now, lost in a wilderness of his own making, he wondered if he'd strayed too far from the Lord's path to ever find his way back.

Chapter Three

The first hint Evan's day was beginning came not from the blare of an alarm, but from the persistent snuffle of a pig. With a snort and a huff, a damp snout pressed against his face.

Halfway incoherent from the lack of sleep, he blinked his eyes open. "Stop it."

Releasing a grunt, the pig persisted. Relentless in its mission, it probed harder with a wet twitchy nose.

He flung out an arm. "Go on, Hambone. Shoo!" Waving the animal away, he rolled over onto his back. Whether or not he wanted to, it was time to get up.

Mission accomplished, the swine let out a satisfied oink and trotted off. Nosing its way out the door, it disappeared.

Watching the pig depart, Evan frowned. Not exactly the way he'd planned to wake up, but it was better than the alternative. Mornings, once a haze of hangovers and regret, had taken on a sharper edge. The clarity was brutal, forcing him to confront the precipice he'd been teetering over for years. The blackouts, the lost time, the nights he couldn't remember and the mornings he wished he could forget.

Hitting rock bottom, he knew he'd needed help. After discreetly consulting his physician, he'd undergone a structured withdrawal program. A few aftereffects lingered, but no serious complications had remained.

Three months had passed, and each day was a battle to stay sober. Quitting was the hardest fight of his life. He could still taste the sharp burn of the alcohol on his tongue, still feel the warm numbness it brought, easing the pain of too many years spent staring down the bad guys and into the abyss of his own mistakes.

There has to be a better way...

A surge of remorse filled him. Yes, he knew the answer. He'd always known. He'd simply chosen to overlook it.

An unbidden memory surfaced, that of Isla's young son, Joel. When he'd taken supper with the family, the child had touchingly asked the Lord to watch over him. The purity of that prayer had struck a chord deep inside him.

More images filtered in. The meal with Isla had been pleasant enough. Once the ice had thawed, they'd had a friendly conversation, exchanging pleasantries about their lives. At first, he'd been peeved Owen Bruhn had picked up the pieces.

Had he chosen a different fork in the road, Isla might have been his wife. As it stood, she was just a fond acquaintance. And he was okay with that.

At least, he thought he was.

During their visit, Isla had asked him if he regretted leaving the Amish community. The question had hit hard, and to his surprise, he'd felt a pang so intense it nearly stole his breath. He missed the sense of belonging, the deep, unwavering connection with his church and his people.

But instead of confessing the truth, he'd held it in, determined to maintain the illusion of control. Letting it crack now would mean unraveling everything—his composure, his pride and maybe even his sanity.

His gaze turned toward his nightstand. Maybe it was time to reach for something greater than himself. Part of the twelve steps, after all, was surrendering to a higher power. Admitting his flaws. Seeking help. And, hardest of all, facing those he'd wronged to make things right.

Reaching out, he pulled open the drawer. A Bible lay inside. He hadn't opened it in years, not since the day he'd watched helplessly as his young sister's life slipped away.

Why? The sights and sounds of the incident still haunted him.

Nothing would ever erase the tragedy. Back then, the Bible's assurances about God's plan had seemed to be a cruel joke. Conviction crumbling, he'd turned away from his beliefs. Still, witnessing the response of police and other emergency responders that day had ignited something inside him—a desire to set things right when they had gone wrong. It was then he'd realized what he wanted to do with his life.

The shrill buzz of his alarm pierced the morning air. A dull ache thudded behind his temples, a warning that a long, demanding day lay ahead. His shifts often bled into overtime, swallowed by paperwork and endless administrative tasks. The extra workload kept him in the field more than he liked, but until new deputies were hired, most of the burden rested on his shoulders.

Releasing a sigh, Evan slid the drawer shut. *Maybe tomorrow.*

Rising to his feet, he fumbled toward the adjoining bathroom. Leaning against the sink, he squinted at his reflection in the mirror. Dark circles hung under his eyes, and his stubbled face looked older than his thirty-four years. He wasn't living. He was existing.

"This isn't a good look," he muttered, dragging a hand across his face. Nowadays, it was hard to remember the man he used to be, one who believed there was still happiness to be found in this world.

Fingers fumbling with the faucet, he splashed cold water on his face, hoping to shock himself into some semblance of alertness. Gradually, the water warmed. Taking soap and washcloth in hand, he scrubbed away the remnants of sleep and yesterday's mistakes. Today he would do better. Moving forward was the only way he knew how to survive.

Twenty minutes later, he'd managed to get himself ready for the day. Despite his growing disillusionment with the job, quitting never crossed his mind. As he buttoned his shirt, the smell of freshly brewed coffee and other breakfast foods wafted through the air.

Busy with her cooking, Aunt Hazel bustled about. Silvery hair covered by a prim *kapp*, she wore a simple but practical frock and sensible black boots. An apron with a tear at one corner circled her plump waist.

Hazel hummed softly as she flipped pancakes on the griddle. Nearby, her pet raccoon, Stewart, was busily engaged sorting through a bowl of fruits and nuts. The creature's masked face and nimble paws made for quite a sight. Always hungry, Hambone snuffled up the bites the raccoon found unacceptable. A rather large orange tomcat sat nearby, licking its paw.

Evan eyed the unlikely group. Settling into the new place had been a shock to his system, especially since he'd only been there a month. The chaotic whirlwind of Hazel's household presented a new challenge every day, testing his patience and adaptability in the strange world she called home.

Having outlived a husband and two *sohn*s, Hazel had chosen not to remarry. Instead, she'd devoted herself to the study of organic medicinal remedies. In her spare time, she rehabbed orphaned animals, caring for a variety of critters. Her presence commanded respect, and folks valued her knowledge to heal using the resources nature provided.

Now seventy-seven, Hazel had always been a force of nature. But her age had begun to challenge her fierce independence. It wasn't safe for her to live alone, prompting a more supportive living arrangement. Since no one else had offered to step up, the responsibility had fallen into his lap by default. Despite her eccentric ways, his great-aunt held a special place in his heart. She was one of the few family members who hadn't turned against him after he went *Englisch*.

Reluctant to startle her, he cleared his throat. "Morning, Hazel."

Hazel turned. "*Guten morgen*," she replied, scooping the pancakes into a tall stack. "I hope Hambone didn't bother you."

"Got my usual nose in the face, right on time."

"I told him to let you sleep." Tsking, Hazel carried the plate to the table. "Breakfast is ready if you'd care for a bite."

His stomach twisted. That much food was more than he could handle so early in the morning.

"A cup of coffee is all I have time for," he said, checking his watch.

"Are you feeling bad? I've never seen a man look so peaked."

Evan swiped a hand through his tousled hair. "I'm just tired." Someday he hoped he'd feel human again. Today, however, wasn't that day.

"If you say so."

He fidgeted, the shadow of his past addiction hanging heavily between them, shattering the illusion of the strong, dependable nephew she had believed in.

"I quit. You know that."

"I do. And I'm proud you're managing."

"But?"

"I think you should get some help," Hazel said, unwilling to mince words. "Find someone you can talk to, so it won't get all bottled up inside you. You could seek counseling from Bishop Harrison. He leads a group for folks with issues."

"I don't believe anyone Amish would want me there," he said, rejecting the suggestion.

"The fact that church hasn't got a place in your life anymore might be part of the problem."

"Please, not today."

Reluctant to address the matter further, he sought solace in a familiar routine. With deliberate movements, he reached up to the cabinet above the counter and selected a worn ceramic cup, its weight and texture providing a comforting familiarity in his hand.

Walking to the stove, he grasped the percolator, pouring out the steaming brew. The first sip helped chase away his headache. The robust blend had a pleasant flavor, a combination of chocolate and cinnamon with just a hint of sweetness. It was more than just coffee; it was a moment of comfort, a respite from the tension dogging his steps.

Savoring the warmth, Evan wondered if moving in to keep an eye on his elderly aunt was a misstep. Through the last month, Hazel seemed to have turned the tables. Instead of being the caretaker, he'd found himself the recipient of her nurturing gestures. From homemade meals that brought back childhood memories to her keen interest in his daily routines, it felt as though the roles had reversed.

"I'm sorry. I know you're just trying to look out for me."

Wiping her hands, Hazel pursed her lips. "You can't blame me for being worried. I know you're stressed." Concern deepened the lines on her weathered face. "I'm not one to lecture, but maybe it's time to think about doing something else."

Touched, he managed a nod. He'd given the idea some thought, though he'd never truly pursued it. The law had always been his focus, the one realm where absolutes existed, a world where right and wrong were clear-cut, not muddied by uncertainty.

"I'll try to manage better," he said. "It's just…

sometimes it's hard to switch off. Feels like more and more people are set on doing wrong, and someone has to take a stand."

"It's not your job to carry the weight of the world," Hazel said. "The problems you're trying to solve belong in *Gott*'s hands. He is the only One who can make things right."

Evan silently acknowledged her worry. The mounting pressure he felt to fix everything was becoming a burden. The desire to accept his limitations and lean on something greater than himself beckoned. Still, he kept backpedaling. He wasn't ready to deal with the Lord. Not yet.

Before he could respond, his cell phone rang. He glanced at the screen, recognizing the emergency dispatch number. As he hadn't yet done a radio check-in, it was the quickest way to reach him.

"Miller," he answered, listening as the dispatcher's voice came through. The news wasn't good.

"I have to go," he announced, abandoning his cup in the sink. "There's a robbery in progress at the Stoltzfus Bakery."

Worry clouded Hazel's expression. "Promise you'll be careful." The sole beacon of care in his life, she was the only one who truly worried about his safety.

"I'll be okay." Mind racing ahead, Evan gave a distracted wave before dashing to his patrol unit.

The predawn darkness clung to the landscape, shadows stretching long and deep. Sliding behind the wheel, he twisted the key, and the engine roared to life. The SUV vibrated with barely contained power, ready to go.

Shifting into gear, he put the pedal to the metal. "This is going to be the day I catch up with that guy…"

Sheriff Miller had been shot. That's all she knew. That's all anyone knew.

The clatter of hooves echoed against the asphalt as the buggy approached the entrance of Burr Oak's hospital. News of the incident had spread like wildfire, casting a shadow over the peaceful community.

Isla's heart pounded in her chest as she disembarked. The cold, clinical facade of the hospital loomed before her. The last time she'd set foot in this place was to say goodbye to her dying *ehemann*. Riddled with cancer, Owen had drawn his final breath inside the cold, impersonal walls. The bills from his illness had eaten up most all their savings.

Abner Pilcher walked beside her. Her neighbor had been the one to bring the terrible news about Evan, interrupting her alterations of a client's dress. Amidst the financial strain following the robbery, she'd poured all her skill into her craft. Too proud to accept charity, she'd worked longer hours to finish her current commissions.

Now, in the cruelest twist of fate, the man who'd helped bring a sense of security back to her life was fighting for his.

Lord, please let him be all right, she prayed as they headed through the sliding glass doors. They hissed open, revealing a lobby bustling with activity. Staffers moved with urgent purpose.

A tight-knit cadre of officers huddled together, their postures tense and their expressions grim. By the look of them, each man was acutely aware the incident that had befallen their comrade could just as easily happen to any one of them. Their eyes, hardened by years of service, now reflected a shared sense of vulnerability and dread.

Recognizing one of the men who'd assisted after the break-in at her home, Isla paused. During the investigation, she'd found Deputy Lopez to be competent and sympathetic. Trying not to appear intrusive, she attempted to follow the conversation.

"Miller was responding to a robbery at the Stoltzfus Bakery," Lopez said, recounting the tense narrative. "He arrived just as the perp fled the scene in his vehicle. I'm guessing he went in pursuit and pulled him over."

"Don't know what happened after that," a second deputy filled in. "Somehow the culprit got the drop on him. By the time we got there, the subject had fled and Miller was down."

"The sheriff didn't go down without a fight," Lopez added, his voice filled with frustration and anger. "He defended himself."

A man wearing the uniform of a Texas Ranger paused mid-note. "So, the suspect is still out there?"

"Yeah," Lopez said. "We found the vehicle the perp fled in. Turned out to be stolen. There was a lot of blood, too. Hopefully, the other guy got what was coming to him."

"No one's shown up locally with an unexplained injury," another officer filled in. "And we've contacted all clinics and hospitals within a hundred-mile radius to be on the lookout."

"Sounds good," the ranger drawled. "A CSI team will start processing the evidence. If there's viable DNA, we can run it through the system, maybe get a hit on who this guy is."

"That lowlife better hope Miller lives," Lopez declared. "Otherwise, he'll be going down for murder."

A gasp clawed its way up Isla's throat. The deputy's narrative reeled through her mind, leaving her shaken. The gravity of the dangers officers faced in the line of duty pressed down on her. She couldn't fathom the harrowing realities they encountered daily.

Abner tugged at her arm. "Folks like us don't

need to hear things like that," he said, leading her out of earshot. "They've got work to do, so let them get to it."

Isla went willingly. "Of course."

"The best thing we can do is pray," the old man advised.

"*Ja*," she agreed. "We will." But her words felt hollow, inadequate. It wasn't that she doubted *Gott*'s power or goodness. Yet in the depths of her heart, a storm raged. Why would the Lord allow such a cruel twist of fate to befall a kind soul? A week earlier, Evan had been vibrant and full of life; sharing supper at her table, reminiscing about their youth and days long gone. Now, the stark reality of his plight hung heavy in the air, casting shadows over everything she saw and felt.

The Lord gave, and the Lord hath taken away, she reminded herself, finding solace in the bittersweet truth. In moments of joy, the verse was a hymn of gratitude. But in the depths of loss, they became a solemn requiem.

"Isla? Is that you?"

Pivoting on her heel, Isla caught sight of a familiar figure. Recognition flooded in.

"*Tante* Hazel," she said, offering a proper greeting to the older woman.

"Isla," the old woman said, reaching out to give her a quick hug. "I'm happy you came."

"I heard Evan was injured…"

Hazel shook her head, her expression tight with

worry. "I don't know anything yet," she said, her breath catching. "I'm waiting for word now."

"I know they're doing all they can." Isla searched the lobby, expecting to see more of Evan's *familie* members. "Do Jonah and Leah know?"

A grimace tightened Hazel's lips. "*Ja*," she said, speaking in a bitter tone. "They were all here."

"Were?"

"It's best they've gone home," Hazel explained. "Jonah was in a froth, and Leah had to take him away to calm him down."

"Jonah's always been hard-nosed in his views," Abner declared, joining the conversation uninvited. "But if you're not baptized, a man has a right to live as he sees fit. It's a choice we're all allowed when we come of age. Jonah should accept it."

"I've prayed Jonah would lay it down," Hazel said. "But he's kept it going all these years."

"I don't understand how he can be so blind to the goodness in Evan's heart," Isla said.

Tucking his thumbs under his suspenders, Abner rocked back on his heels. "Jonah hails from those Ely's Bluff Amish," he said, speaking of the smaller, lesser-known settlement a stone's throw outside Burr Oak. "They're Old Order folks, and they've got some severe beliefs."

"I will not stop praying for a reconciliation," Hazel continued, her voice breaking.

As they spoke, a surgeon slipped through a set of double doors at the end of a long hallway.

"I'm looking for the Miller family."

Seeing him, Isla's heart skipped a beat. "Here," she said, including herself in the matter. And why shouldn't she? She'd known Evan since they were knee-high to grasshoppers. It was only right she should know what was going on.

Clad in scrubs, the physician walked over. "I'm Dr. Keller," he said, offering a gentle smile. "I had the honor of treating the sheriff. I'm pleased to inform you Evan made it through fine."

"Was it bad?" Abner asked.

"Fortunately, his tactical gear did its job, and there are no internal injuries." Dr. Keller's tense expression relaxed a bit as he spoke. "He'll feel like he's been kicked by a mule, but that should ease up over time. One round penetrated the deltoid region of his shoulder, but the exit wound is clean, and there's no major vascular or nerve damage."

"Praise *Gott*," Hazel said.

"How is he doing?" Isla asked.

Dr. Keller gave a small, wry smile. "He's not thrilled to be here. Agitated and resistant is the best way to describe it."

Hazel nodded. "That's my nephew. Bullheaded and impossible to keep down."

"He lost a lot of blood. We had to sedate him to clean and suture his wound," Dr. Keller said.

"I'd like to keep him under observation for a few days, just to be cautious. After that, he should be able to go home."

Relief flooded Hazel's face. "*Danke*, doctor," she said, reaching for his hand. "*Danke* so much for looking after him."

"Evan's a strong man," Keller continued. "He needs time to process it all, but he should be all right."

"Can I see him?" Hazel asked.

"You can, but only for a few minutes. I'll have a nurse escort you in," Dr. Keller said before departing.

Minutes ticked away, then a nurse finally appeared. "This way, please," she said, ushering the visitors down a quiet hallway.

Reaching the threshold of a block of private rooms, Isla hesitated. "Abner and I can wait here," she said, offering Hazel privacy to visit her great-nephew.

"I'd like you to come, Isla. You've always been a *freundin* to me. It's *gut* to know you still care about Evan, too."

"Of course," she murmured, her voice steady. The nurses and doctors did their best, but Evan needed familiar faces and voices around him.

The nurse guided them toward a set of double doors. "Dr. Keller says you can stay ten minutes," she said, ushering them into the peaceful sanctuary of the private room.

Evan lay unconscious, his right shoulder covered by bandages.

Approaching his bedside, Hazel took his hand in hers. "He's such a *nachdenklicher mann*," she murmured. "He recently moved in to help me with the *haus*. It got to be too much for me to keep up with."

Isla blinked, taken aback. She hadn't known that, hadn't realized he'd made such a quiet sacrifice. But that was exactly the kind of person Evan was. When they were growing up, he was always the first to step in and offer a helping hand.

Overwhelmed, she felt sadness wash over her. "*Liebes herz*," she whispered, addressing him with the private endearment used when they were younger.

The nurse swiftly assessed his vital signs before making a few notes in his chart. "Just another few minutes, please. He needs to rest."

Hazel's eyes shimmered with unshed tears. "I'd like to pray."

"Of course," the nurse murmured, stepping away.

Isla respectfully bowed her head. Silently, she added a plea to *Gott* for a complete healing. Evan had a special place in her heart. He always would. Despite the tumultuous journey of their past, he had once been her best friend and the man she'd dreamed of marrying.

Flooded with regret for lost time and missed

opportunities, she wondered how different things might have been if they could have stayed together. But life had sent them in different directions. Still, she found herself grappling with a mix of emotions. Sadness for what had been lost, and a faint glimmer of hope that maybe, just maybe, there was a reason their paths had crossed again.

Chapter Four

The low hum of the fluorescent lights buzzed in Evan's ears as he lay in the sterile confines of the hospital room. The antiseptic smell of the place did nothing to mask the sour taste of defeat lingering in his gut. His pride throbbed worse than the injury he'd sustained, a sharp reminder of his failure. The physical pain was easy to bear. What stung was the look in Texas Ranger Glen Palmer's eyes, a mixture of suspicion and something that penetrated deeper.

Disappointment.

Palmer's presence commanded respect, and his reputation as a relentless investigator preceded him. But there was no sympathy in that steely blue gaze, only the hard look of a man who demanded answers. And the truth.

"Tell me again how you remember it." Palmer took notes and asked questions in a steady voice, the kind that demanded answers without rising an octave.

The quiet command lingered in the air, pressing down on Evan as he fought to keep his composure. A day had passed since the shooting, and Palmer had arrived with a barrage of questions about the sequence of events. The third retelling was just as excruciating as the first.

"Like I told you, I got the call around 5:15 in the morning. Dispatch relayed there was a robbery in progress at Stoltzfus Bakery."

"Go on."

"As I was heading to the scene, a pickup blasted through a stop sign. The description fit, so I went in pursuit. My lights set him off, and the driver sped up. Thankfully, there wasn't anyone out that early."

"I see." Palmer jotted a few notes on a legal pad. "Continue, please."

"The suspect fled toward the edge of town and then veered onto a utility road." He paused, trying to recall every detail. He remembered the flash of brake lights, the screech of tires, the cloud of dust as the truck swerved off the asphalt and onto gravel.

"And?" Palmer prompted.

"He was going too fast, couldn't make the turn. The truck ended up in a ditch. I pulled over and figured he'd try to run. I didn't expect him to come out shooting."

Palmer's gaze didn't waver. "Why do you think that is?"

The question hung in the air.

"It was still dark, and dirt and gravel were flying," he replied after a moment. "I thought I was fast to respond. But I wasn't fast enough."

"Not fast enough," Palmer echoed, his tone flat. "A lawman is supposed to have quick reflexes and a sharp eye. What do you think slowed you down?"

Evan's mouth went dry. He didn't want to say it, didn't want to admit what he feared most. But he knew Palmer wasn't going to let it go.

"I was tired," he finally confessed. "I've been working extra shifts. And I've also been dealing with personal issues. I—I wasn't as sharp as I should've been."

Palmer's eyes narrowed. "Is there anything else that might have hindered your reflexes?"

Evan inwardly winced. His recent wound burned, but not as much as the insinuation he knew was coming. He'd been waiting for it, dreading it. "Absolutely not."

"You want to think about that and answer again?"

"What are you getting at, Glen?"

Palmer leaned in, his voice lowering. "How much did you have to drink before you went out?"

The question felt heavy and suffocating.

"I wasn't hungover if that's what you're implying."

Palmer didn't back down, his gaze piercing. "That's not what I've heard."

Evan's pulse thudded, each beat a reminder of the truth he'd tried so hard to bury. He'd had a problem, a bad one that had shadowed him for years. Despite it all, he'd put on a mask of professionalism, determined to perform his duties with competence. He was only human, and like everyone else, he'd stumbled and fallen more times than he cared to admit. But this time he could answer with a clear conscience.

"You heard wrong. I quit. Not a drop has passed my lips in months. And it has never affected my ability to do my job."

Palmer let out a slow breath, his expression unreadable. "You sure about that? Because from my point of view, being slow on the draw almost got you killed."

Shame washed over him, a bitter wave that threatened to pull him under. He'd spent his life upholding the law, protecting others. But he hadn't been able to protect himself, from the bullet or the bottle.

Failure clawed at him. He believed he'd hidden his flaws from the prying eyes of the public, but the gossip had gotten around. It always did.

Don't let the bad things win, he silently reminded himself.

"I'm telling the truth." Yet even as the words left his mouth, the ghost of his former addiction arose, resurrecting the feel of cool glass against his palm and the searing burn of whiskey sliding down his throat. Quitting was the hardest thing he'd ever done. But he had no regrets. He'd done it for the love of a dear old woman who still believed he was a hero.

Palmer's tone softened, but the edge remained. "I need to know I can trust you. That the people of this town can trust you. If you've still got a problem, we can deal with it now. But if you lie to me, we can't come back from that."

"I'm sober as a judge, and I intend to stay that way."

The older man studied him, the silence between them heavy.

"Okay…" he finally allowed. "For now, I'll take it at face value. Later, I'll see what Dr. Rhyland has to say. You'll be contacted when you're scheduled to see him."

"Fair enough." After a shooting, a mandatory psychological evaluation was required. Knowing that, he was prepared to undergo all required examinations. The road ahead would be paved with difficult questions and the need for brutal honesty.

"We'll move on," Palmer said, tapping his pen against the pad. "What else do you remember?"

Evan winced as memories of the incident unspooled across his mind's screen, vivid and unrelenting. The echo of that day's chaos still haunted him. "As for the man who shot me, I didn't see his face. But I saw the gun the moment he swung out of the truck."

"Go on," Palmer urged.

Evan's breath hitched as he relived his split-second decision, the feel of his weapon in his hand, the tension in the air thick with danger. And then, the impact of three bullets striking his chest in rapid succession. The memory of those shots, so sharp and sudden, had burned itself into his mind. The deafening crack of the shots still rang in his ears, as did the acrid odor of gunpowder. It wasn't just pain that followed; it was as if a sledgehammer had slammed into him. The sensation had been so powerful, so overwhelming, that for a split second, he'd thought it was the end. But then there was the dull, reassuring pressure of his body armor, the lifesaving shield that had taken the brunt of the blows and kept him breathing.

"After those bullets hit, everything's a blur." Shaking his head, he added, "I was sure my aim was good, but I must have been wrong."

Lips going flat, Palmer glanced up from his writing. "It was good."

Evan blinked, processing the unexpected revelation. "Did I—"

"Kill him?" Palmer finished.

Evan froze. As the lawman involved in the shooting, he was acutely aware of the protocols that came into play. Standard procedure dictated that any officer who discharged their weapon in the line of duty would be subjected to intense scrutiny, treated almost as a suspect rather than a protector.

"I can't answer that," Palmer said, setting his pen aside and leaning back into his chair with a weary sigh. "The stolen vehicle was recovered, and we found blood. There were signs the perp was wounded. Despite the evidence, we haven't found him."

"Any prints?"

Palmer frowned. "Nothing clear enough to be useful. All we have is unknowns. Somehow, he got away clean."

"It's been like chasing a shadow. He's always one step ahead."

"This guy is organized and professional," Palmer mused. "The fact that you got as close as you did might have shaken him. I wouldn't be surprised if he decides to hide out. A close call like this might even prompt him to move on to a different location."

"That doesn't sound good for the next town he lands in."

Palmer spread his hands, indicating the uncertainty that still surrounded the case. "We can only do what we can do."

Evan settled back against the pillows. "Wish I wasn't stuck here." Enforced confinement to the hospital felt far worse than the lingering physical pain. "I'd like to get back to work."

"That's not going to happen, and you know it.

As of right now, you are on administrative leave," Palmer said, his tone firm.

Knowing the protocols, Evan sighed. "Guess I knew it was coming." Even though he believed his actions were justified, there were other complexities to be considered. First and foremost would be *was he fit for duty*? His physical recovery, mental well-being and other factors would also be considered.

"Deputy Lopez will be stepping into the sheriff's role until further notice," Palmer said, closing his briefcase with a soft click. "In the meantime, I'll assist the investigation into the robberies that led up to the incident. If anything comes to mind, no matter how small, get in touch with me."

"Understood."

The ranger departed. As the door swung shut behind him, the room felt colder and emptier.

Evan stared at the ceiling, the confines of the room pressing down on him. He already knew the review of his activities would be thorough, impartial and relentless. Kept at arm's length from the proceedings, he was reduced to the role of an observer.

The wait would be excruciating. He had no doubt he'd acted with justifiable force. Yet, doubt remained. Had his troubles compromised his ability to perform his role as a lawman?

The final verdict would either vindicate him— or change the course of his career forever.

* * *

Isla kneaded the dough for apple dumplings as the late afternoon light filtered through the curtains, casting a warm glow over Hazel's kitchen. The scent of yeast and cinnamon mingled with the aroma of chicken stew simmering on the stove.

Hambone snuffled around her skirt. His ears flopped comically as he nudged for treats. Nearby, Stewart, the raccoon, perched on a low shelf, his nimble fingers working over a piece of fruit he'd pilfered from the apple basket.

Chuckling over the old woman's unusual menagerie, Isla tried to focus on her task. Hard as she tried to stay focused, her thoughts kept drifting back to Evan. Released from medical supervision, he was scheduled to come home. Knowing how overwhelmed Hazel was, she'd offered to help with tidying up and preparing a special meal to ease her burden.

It's the right thing to do, she reminded herself. She owed Evan a favor and she intended to follow through.

Glancing out the kitchen window, she caught sight of Joel and Olivia, who she'd sent out to play while she helped Hazel for the afternoon. The old property sat serenely on the outskirts of town, a sprawling acre surrounded by tall oak and maple trees. Wildflowers and thick, tangled underbrush provided a natural boundary, creating a private haven. A pair of old wooden barns stood nearby, their weathered exteriors home to the livestock. Chickens roamed within the perimeters of their pens, while a few goats nibbled the grass.

Busy arranging the table, Hazel set out her good stoneware, the ones reserved for special occasions. "How are the dumplings coming along?" she asked.

Isla pressed her hands into the dough, shaping it. "It's been a while since I've made them, but I recall they were Evan's favorite dessert."

Hazel's eyes sparkled with affection. "You're too kind, dear. It means a lot that he will come home to a hearty meal and familiar faces." Beaming, she added, "I'll be happy to have him back, safe and sound."

"Me, too. Though I must admit, I was surprised when you told me he's living here now."

"My nephew was the only one who cared to check on me," Hazel said, her voice carrying that familiar, chatty tone. "You know, when I took that fall a few months back, it was Evan who came. No one else in the *familie* bothered."

Isla gasped. "That's dreadful!"

"That's the way the Miller side is," Hazel said, waving her hands in a dismissive gesture. "They've never treated me like kin."

"But you were married to Jonah's *Onkel* Gideon," Isla exclaimed. "That should count for something."

"Things changed after Gideon passed," Hazel

admitted, voice faltering. "Now I'm just a *kinder-lose alte frau*, a burden to everyone."

"You are not!" Isla scolded, wiping her hands on a clean cloth before covering the dough and setting it aside to rest. "You're not a burden."

"Jonah doesn't think so," Hazel confessed. "He's always been upset I kept in touch with Evan after he left the church." Shaking her head, she added. "I couldn't kick the *boi* aside when he was struggling to make something of himself in the *Englisch* world."

Isla ached with empathy. She couldn't begin to fathom the crushing weight of losing the support of the very people who were supposed to be his foundation. The challenges must have been overwhelming for an eighteen-year-old, the harsh judgment of a strict parent weighing down his steps. Despite the odds, Evan had found the courage to carve out his own path.

"I'm glad you were there for him," she said. "He's a *gut* man. And I know he's happy to be here for you, now."

"I don't know what I would have done if he hadn't made the offer." Sniffing, Hazel retrieved a handkerchief out of her apron pocket. "He's been so kind, so patient. He wants to work on the *haus*, fix this old place up." Dabbing at her eyes, she eyed the kitchen, taking in its dated features. "I've no one to leave the property to, so he'll inherit it."

"But not for a long time." Reaching out, Isla offered a comforting embrace. "It sounds like Evan is right where he needs to be. And so are you."

Hazel's lips trembled with emotion. "I believe *Gott* sent him to remind me that *familie* isn't just about blood. It's about who shows up when you need them most."

Isla pressed her lips together. The familiar pang of longing gripped her. She'd battled with herself, caught between respecting Evan's need for space and the overpowering urge to be there for him. The conflict had been relentless, but in the end, her need to offer support had won out.

If only he'd needed me enough back then to stay.

"Do you think it was proper?" she blurted.

Hazel's brow furrowed in confusion. "If what was proper?"

"Going to see him," she clarified, her voice wavering. "I mean, we haven't been close in years."

"How did you feel about it?"

"Terrified. Just a week ago, he was fixing my door after the break-in. He had supper at my table. And then…just like that, he almost lost his life." She paused, her voice thick with emotion. "I couldn't bear the thought of not being there when I heard what had happened. But now I wonder if I had any right to step in the way I did."

"If you felt compelled to be there, then it was the right thing to do." Hazel reached out, placing a reassuring hand on Isla's arm. "My nephew has a lot of regrets. You've always been one of them."

Isla started. "I—I didn't know."

The older woman took a hesitant step back. "I shouldn't have said anything," she murmured, returning to her stove. She lifted the lid on the pot, giving the hearty stew a comforting stir. "I'm grateful that you were there to lend your prayers."

"Do you think we could be friends again?"

"*Ja*, of course. It's never too late for healing, or forgiveness."

Isla wouldn't say it out loud, but she did still care for Evan. She was here because a part of her had never let go of the past, had never stopped wondering what might have been if he'd chosen her over the *Englisch* world beyond their small community.

"I just want him to be happy."

"Don't forget about your own happiness," Hazel said. "You deserve that too."

"Do I?" Unsure she believed it, Isla turned back to the dessert she'd promised to make. After pressing out the dough and spooning in the filling, she slid the dumplings into the oven. Needing to keep her hands busy, she grabbed a broom to sweep up the flour she'd spilled. The simple, repetitive motion brought her a moment to think while she wrestled with emotions she'd believed were long gone. Unfortunately, they were not.

Food prepared, Hazel surveyed their handiwork

with a satisfied smile. "I think we're done. And just in time."

Isla glanced toward the clock hanging on the wall. Ten after six and nearly time for supper. "Who's picking him up?"

"One of the deputies was supposed to bring him home," Hazel answered.

Just then, the sound of tires crunching on the gravel outside signaled the arrival they had been waiting for.

Isla glanced toward the large bay windows, her attention snagging on the county patrol cruiser as it eased to a stop just outside.

"Oh, my! They've arrived!" With a flurry of anxious energy, Hazel shooed Hambone and his raccoon companion out of the kitchen. "Go, both of you!"

Hambone oinked back, stubbornly holding his place.

"Oh, no, you don't!" With a swift motion, Hazel gave the pig a firm push with her foot. "You're not to be in when people are eating," she insisted, letting the pair out into the backyard.

Giving up, Hambone trotted outside. The raccoon skittered behind.

Isla felt a smile tug at her lips. Hazel was a licensed wildlife rehabber. Whenever a wild animal was found injured or in distress, Hazel was called in.

Shaking her head, Hazel latched the screen

with a soft click. "They both beg so dreadfully you can't get a single bite." Kitchen peaceful once more, she glanced toward the living room. "Would you mind getting the door? I'm not sure Evan has his key."

"Not at all," Isla murmured. She smoothed a few stray locks of hair that had slipped free from the confines of her *kapp*. It was a simple gesture, but one that steadied her nerves as she prepared for whatever was to come. When she reached for the handle, her breath caught in her throat. She hesitated, gathering the courage she wasn't sure she had.

And then, there he was.

Evan stepped onto the porch, his figure framed by the fading light of the late afternoon. Deputy Lopez followed close behind.

"I didn't expect to see you here," Evan said, a hint of surprise threading his voice.

Isla summoned a smile. "I've been helping Hazel with a few things." Gathering her composure, she stepped aside to let him pass. "She's been waiting all day."

"We could've been here hours ago, but it took forever to get discharged," Deputy Lopez groused.

Evan removed his hat as he stepped inside, offering a nod of gratitude. "Thank you for lending a hand."

"Of course."

Conversation dropped off. They just stood

there, awkwardly staring at each other. The echo of silence between them seemed to amplify the weight of his recent ordeal. The violence he'd endured had left its mark, etching a deeper weariness into his features. His face was leaner, sharper. But it was his eyes that had truly changed. His gaze held a deeper intensity—pain, and something else she couldn't quite identify.

Taking in the transformation, Isla instinctively pressed a hand against her nervous middle. Despite his quiet strength, Evan's posture was that of a man whose resilience was more a necessity than a choice. A weary warrior, he appeared to be carrying burdens too heavy for one soul.

Unable to meet his gaze any longer, she turned away. Anxiety tightened in her chest, not only for the pain he'd endured, but for the abyss he seemed to be teetering on the edge of. She yearned to mend his wounds but didn't know how or where to begin.

Desperate, she sent out a silent plea. *How do I help him, Lord?*

Chapter Five

Evan stood in the dimly lit bathroom, the smell of mildew hanging in the air. Unused since his Uncle Gideon passed, the years of neglect had taken a toll. The tiles, once white, were now an unappealing shade of yellow, and the faded wallpaper was peeling. A slow leak behind the sink meant everything would have to be torn out and replaced.

He sighed, wincing slightly as the movement tugged at his healing shoulder. "Okay, let's see if we can make something of this disaster," he muttered, grabbing a wrench from the toolbox.

Just as he began to remove the ancient faucet, a loud snort echoed through the narrow hallway. He turned his head in time to see Hambone saunter in. The pig snuffled before nudging his leg with its snout, demanding attention.

"Not now," he grumbled, trying to push the intruder away with his foot.

Hambone was relentless, shoving his round body against Evan's knee until he stumbled back, narrowly avoiding falling into the empty tub.

Stewart made his entrance next. The raccoon clambered up onto the counter with an agility that belied his plump frame, chattering as he inspected the tools Evan had laid out. The animal's tiny paws grasped a roll of duct tape before darting away, his stolen treasure in tow. Crafty and intelligent, Stewart loved stealing things to add to his stash.

"Give that back!" Frustration filled him as he watched the raccoon disappear. "Great. Just great." He didn't feel like chasing the animal, so let the little thief go. Later, he would retrieve all the things Stewart had filched.

Giving Hambone another nudge, he set to his task with determination. The bathroom needed a complete overhaul, and he intended to strip it down to the studs and remodel it from the ground up. He wasn't a natural handyman, but watching instructional videos had given him enough confidence to tackle the project. He'd already picked out all the new fittings: a sleek vanity with double sinks, modern fixtures in brushed nickel, and a spacious walk-in shower with glass doors to replace the old, stained bathtub.

It was a lot to take on for his first project, but he refused to be deterred. The idea of sitting around with nothing to do during his enforced leave was unbearable. He needed something he could throw himself into with all the focus and intensity he normally reserved for his job.

A twinge in his shoulder halted his progress. In the back of his mind, he knew it wasn't just about keeping busy. Deep down, he was desperate to avoid the one thing that kept flickering in the back of his mind.

A suspect had tried to kill him.

And he'd come close to succeeding.

"Don't think about it." But he couldn't stop. The memories refused to go away. The sight of the perp's gun, the sound of shots ringing out and the impact of each strike against his body armor kept replaying across his mind's screen.

The fine hairs on the back of his neck rose even as a shiver curled around his spine. He blew out a breath, trying to dispel the remnants of anxiety and disbelief.

Truth be told, he'd been caught off guard. He was used to dealing with lost sheep and minor disputes, not life-threatening encounters. His gear had saved him, but his heart still raced when he thought about how close he'd come to a different kind of reckoning. He replayed the moment he'd drawn his weapon, the adrenaline surging through him as he attempted to defend himself. It was a split-second decision, one that had seemed to stretch into an eternity.

You made it through.

No, more was on the line than that. He had always prided himself on keeping his community safe. Now, it wasn't. Burr Oak had always been a sanctuary of calm, an oasis far removed from issues plaguing larger cities. The last few years had changed that. Crime had begun to seep into their way of life, staining the once-quiet community. Now, the familiar seemed tainted by the intrusion.

A sigh winnowed past his lips, laden with a sense of foreboding. He still couldn't process a suspect who would choose to gun down a cop in cold blood to avoid getting caught. The bullet that had struck his shoulder was more than an injury; it was a stark reminder of his narrow escape from death. The lingering pain served as a constant reminder of how fragile life could be.

Evan brushed a hand across his mouth. Each passing moment deepened the ache for a drink.

He steeled his resolve. *Not going to happen.*

Not today. Or any other.

"Lord, please keep me sober and on track."

It wasn't much. Just a whispered plea from a man too far gone to expect an answer. But it was a start.

Pushing aside his somber thoughts, Evan refocused on the task at hand. He set about dismantling the vanity, detaching the mounting bolts before lifting the sink away from its place. He placed it on the floor, revealing the connections beneath.

Kneeling, he inspected the exposed pipes, preparing to disconnect them. He unscrewed the slip nuts on the P-trap with his hand, allowing the piece to fall away. He then loosened the nuts connecting the sink's tailpiece to the drainpipe.

Just as he began to tackle the main water supply connections, Hambone rooted in to help.

"Go away." Pushing the pig aside, he focused on the water lines, using a wrench to twist the fittings free. As he applied pressure to the wrench, the connection gave way with a sudden gush of cold water.

Startled, Hambone let out a squeal. The pig darted out of the bathroom in a flurry of hooves and indignant grunts.

Evan scrambled to shut off the valve. Once the flow stopped, he wiped the water from his face and surveyed the mess. The bathroom floor was now a small pool. Snagging a handful of old rags, he mopped up the mess.

Aunt Hazel appeared at the doorway. Lips pursed, she surveyed the sopping floor. "Oh, my. What happened?"

"Beats me," he said, shaking his head. "I thought I turned off the main water line to the house."

Hazel's usual cheerful expression shifted. "Oh, dear. I turned it back on to make lunch." As if to excuse her forgetful actions, she extended the tray she carried. A glass of iced tea was accompanied by a thick sandwich and homemade cookies, their edges golden brown. "I thought you might be hungry, so I made you something to eat."

Evan's annoyance faded. A rumbling stomach reminded him he hadn't eaten since breakfast. Accepting her peace offering, he took a bite. Tender roast beef slathered with mayo on fresh wheat bread. It was delicious.

"Thanks for the food."

"You're welcome, dear." Hazel glanced around, her gaze lingering on the disarray. "I have to say, it's *gut* to see you taking care of the property. I thought about selling after Gideon and the *boi*s passed, but I just couldn't bring myself to let it go. Too many memories, I guess." Her voice softened, a hint of nostalgia creeping in. "This place is all I have left of them."

Twelve years had passed since the accident that had stolen Hazel's husband and sons. Evan had been fresh out of the academy then, a rookie deputy assigned the grim task of helping to recover their bodies. Caught in a grain silo, all three men had been engulfed, a danger of farm life. The tragedy had left Hazel on the outskirts of the family. In the absence of others, he'd made it his duty to stay close to his great-aunt.

"It's a fine old house," he said. "I just need to get it back in shape."

"You need more than that," Hazel said, her eyes softening with a touch of sadness. "You need a *familie*. A *fraa*. *Kinder*."

She wasn't wrong. The house was too big for

just two people. Too empty. But the life she spoke of felt just as out of reach as it always had.

"That's something I'll think about after the work is done." He stood and handed her the empty plate, forcing a smile. "For now, I better head to the hardware store. I need to pick up a few things."

Hazel perked up. "Then you'll be going out?"

"That's the plan. Why? You need anything?"

"I do have an errand. If you don't mind."

"Sure. Anything."

"Could you drop by Isla's house? She left her shawl, and I'd like to return it. I'd also like to send her a few things from the pantry to thank her for helping while you were in the hospital."

Though he believed he was on decent terms with Isla, there had been an underlying current in their last encounter that he couldn't quite place. It wasn't hostility, but it was more than mere reserve. They'd managed to smile and nod at each other, but conversation had been strained. Polite but distant was the best way to describe it.

"I could do that, if you think she'd be okay with it."

"I don't see why she would mind," Hazel said. "She's been there for you when others haven't. She came to the hospital the day you were injured."

"Really?"

"*Ja*. She's been praying, too. For your recovery, and that you would find your way back to *Gott*."

"I didn't think she'd care one way or another," he said, attempting to mask his discomfort behind the flippant remark.

"Well, you were mistaken," Hazel replied. "She does, and she always has. Far more than you realize."

Stunned into silence, Evan's gaze dropped to the worn, damp floorboards. He'd been so consumed by his own turmoil that he hadn't fully appreciated Isla's gentle presence. Her smile, her laughter and the warmth of her presence were as vivid as if she were standing right in front of him.

A faint tremor coursed through him, a physical manifestation of the emotional upheaval he'd been trying to suppress. The realization he still harbored feelings for her was both painful and enlightening, a stark contrast to the numbness that had enveloped his life. However, the poignant memories also served as a biting reminder of all he had relinquished.

It was also a part of his past that was presently out of his reach.

Isla sat at her desk in the parlor. The soft light of the afternoon sun flickered through the blinds, casting its light on the pile of bills she'd recently received. A stark reminder of the violent break-in that had left her finances in shambles—none could be paid in full. Yet not even one could be ignored, either.

Sifting through the stack, her gaze darted between each one as she jotted down the balances owed. There was the monthly propane bill, a constant expense that couldn't go unpaid. Next, she noted the recent dental work for Olivia, a necessary but unexpected cost. And on top of it all, the bill for thread and fabric. The supplies were essential to keep her sewing business afloat. Each figure seemed to weigh heavier as she tried to prioritize the most urgent needs.

A profound sense of isolation gripped her, tightening her throat with a raw, unspoken ache. She hadn't asked for help. But the neighbors knew, as they always seemed to, when someone in the community was struggling. That was the Amish way: silent, but present. Through the last week, gift baskets had appeared on her porch. Most of the items had been edible, helping to stretch the dwindling stock in her pantry.

Now and again, an envelope with a few bills stuffed inside accompanied the offerings. A ten here, a twenty there. The money was helpful, but it wasn't enough. The loss of her savings was a heavy burden. Coupled with the sense of violation—knowing a strange man had entered her home, rifling through her things—the theft had left her feeling vulnerable and exposed.

Overwhelmed, she set down her pen and

leaned forward, steepling her hands as she closed her eyes.

"Lord, You know my heart, and You see my struggles. Please, help me carry this." Even as life's harsh realities pressed in, she held fast to the belief that *Gott*'s mercy and guidance would never fail her.

Her prayer had barely ended when an insistent knock announced a visitor's arrival.

Startled, Isla glanced out the window, her eyes falling on a familiar vehicle parked near the front gate. A flood of relief swept over her. After days of anxious prayers, someone had finally come to collect their commission.

"Praise to you, *Gott*," she breathed, the faint glimmer of hope rekindling in her tired heart. Quickly tucking away her paperwork, she adjusted her *kapp* and apron before opening the door with a welcoming smile.

"Miss Richards," she greeted warmly. "I'm so happy to see you. Please, come in."

Andrea Richards walked in with an air of effortless elegance. Dressed in a sleek, tailored suit, her hair styled to perfection, the *Englisch* woman was a stark contrast to the modest surroundings.

"Good afternoon, Mrs. Bruhn," she greeted with a warm smile. "I'm here to pick up my dresses."

"They're all finished, altered just the way you requested," she said, inviting her customer into her sewing room. "I have them ready for you."

"I hope you didn't think I forgot you," Andrea remarked as they walked. "I meant to come sooner, but I got so busy with work."

"I understand," Isla said, stepping to the rack where she'd hung the dresses. "There's always plenty to tend to. The days don't leave much room for idleness."

Taking down the ones she needed, she carefully laid them out, showcasing the finished product. Preserving the original sophistication of the styles, she'd performed each alteration with meticulous care.

Her client's eyes sparkled as she examined the garments, her delight evident. "These are perfect," she exclaimed, holding the dresses to her shoulders and twirling with enthusiasm. "I can't wait to wear them. You've truly outdone yourself."

"Would you like to try them on?" Isla gestured toward the cozy dressing room tucked discreetly to the side. "I can check how they fit and make any final adjustments."

Andrea glanced at her watch, a delicate gold piece. "I'm on my break and running behind, so I'll have to decline."

"If the dresses don't fit, just bring them back anytime." Pleased her client was satisfied, she meticulously folded each garment, smoothing out wrinkles before carefully placing each between layers of pristine white tissue paper. Tucked into a flat garment box, they were ready to go.

Andrea opened her designer purse, revealing its sleek interior. "How much do I owe?" As she unzipped her wallet, a thick stack of bills appeared.

Anxiety lingering from the recent theft, Isla felt her palms turn clammy. The sheer volume of the notes Andrea Richards so casually carried pulled her thoughts in different directions: how she would manage such a sum, the responsibility it entailed and the very real danger of walking around with it.

"Um, fifty dollars per dress," she replied. "One hundred and fifty in total."

"This should cover it." Andrea's fingers moved with precision as she plucked out two hundred-dollar notes. "I'm adding fifty more to cover the time you had to wait to be paid. I hope that's okay." Voice steady and confident, her gaze didn't waver as she handed over the cash.

Isla folded the money with care, her fingers brushing the worn fabric of her apron as she tucked them securely into her pocket. The crisp new currency and her client's fine attire highlighted the stark difference between their worlds.

"The extra is very welcome," she said, grateful for the unexpected blessing.

Andrea glanced at her watch again, a touch of urgency in her demeanor. "I hate to rush off, but

I really should get back to the office. Thank you for all your hard work."

Isla followed her into the foyer. "If you happen to know anyone who could use sewing services, I'd be thankful if you could send them my way."

"Oh, absolutely. Your work on my dresses has been impeccable. I'll tell everyone I know, Mrs. Bruhn. You deserve the recognition for your talent."

"*Danke.* Your recommendation means a lot."

"I'll happily spread the word about your shop. I love passing my blessings along to others," Andrea said, offering her hand. "I can't say how much knowing you has added to my life."

An odd thing to say, but surely well-intentioned.

Before Isla could respond, a new visitor knocked at the door.

Who could that be?

"Excuse me," she said, offering a polite nod before hurrying to answer it.

Evan stood on her porch. "Good afternoon," he said, tipping his cowboy hat. "I hope I'm not interrupting." His private vehicle, a sleek dual-cab pickup, was parked at the curb. Dressed in casual clothes—jeans, a shirt and work boots—his shoulders were relaxed.

"Not at all," she replied.

He extended his hand, presenting the shawl she'd recently misplaced. "Hazel asked me to drop this off." Only his gaze hinted the errand was more of an obligation than a favor, and it showed in the subtle tension around his eyes.

Isla had no chance to claim it before another voice interrupted their exchange.

"Sheriff!" Andrea Richards exclaimed. "It's good to see you're back on your feet. I was so worried when I heard you'd been injured. I meant to come by the hospital, but I didn't want to be a bother." Juggling the box, she offered him an awkward hug. "I hope you're better."

Evan returned a shrug as he pulled away. "Thanks. I am. Just taking things one day at a time."

"I'm so glad you're recovering," Andrea continued, her voice rising an octave with excitement. "I was on pins and needles hoping you wouldn't let the injury get the best of you. Your dedication is truly inspiring."

"I was just doing my job," he said.

Andrea brightened. "We'll have to get together for lunch. Then you can tell me all about it."

"Maybe." Offering a polite smile, he made no attempt to follow through with a firm commitment. "Depends how things go."

"I'm holding you to it," Andrea giggled, a flirtatious sparkle in her eye. "Guess I'd better get back to the office." She gave a playful wave and added, "Bye, all," before prancing down the sidewalk.

Isla winced as Andrea carelessly tossed the box

into the trunk before sliding behind the wheel of her snazzy convertible. The engine roared to life, and the vehicle zoomed away, leaving a trail of exhaust and a cloud of dust.

Despite the much-needed payment, she was relieved to see her client depart. Something about her didn't sit right. But it wasn't just Andrea. Evan's familiar greeting to the woman tugged at something deep inside.

How did they know each other? And why did it bother her so much?

Frown deepening, Isla looked back to the unexpected visitor taking up space on her porch. Their last encounter had been charged and left too much hanging between them. The memory of unsaid words and stolen glances stirred her emotions.

If we don't settle things now, she thought, *we never will*.

Chapter Six

❧

"I hope coming by didn't take you out of your way," Isla said, setting down two tall glasses of iced tea on the patio table. Hazel's cookies accompanied the drinks. She took a seat, her gaze lingering on him for a moment. "How have you been?"

Evan sank into one of the wicker chairs, stretching his long legs. "Getting along. Getting things done."

"I don't suppose you have any news?"

"About the thief?" he asked.

"*Ja.*"

"Nothing so far. Glen Palmer promised he'd keep me updated, but I haven't heard a peep." His voice was steady, but there was an edge of frustration beneath it.

An uneasy weight settled over her. "I've prayed he would be caught."

"You're not the only one," he said, frowning deeply. "I'd sleep a lot better if he was behind bars."

Goose bumps prickled along her arms. Knowing the thief hadn't been apprehended made it hard to feel safe. All she could do was cling to her faith in *Gott*'s plan, trusting that justice would come, not just for her, but for all who had endured. Not just for herself, but for all those who had suffered.

Especially Evan.

There was a guardedness about him, a lingering tension that hinted at scars deeper than the one the bullet had inflicted. She saw it in the tightness around his eyes, in the way he forced a smile.

Looking at him now, she longed to reach out. "How's your shoulder?"

Flexing his arm, he winced. "Doing pretty good. I'm going to physical therapy, and that helps a lot."

She smiled. "I'm happy to hear it."

"I meant to stop by sooner," he said. "I've been wanting to check in on you and the kids."

"Mercifully, I'm getting along." Her smile faltered, but she held it in place, hoping it was convincing. Unfortunately, her ends weren't meeting. The money she'd received wouldn't stretch far at all. Each passing day brought a new worry, adding another failure to the growing pile.

Conversation ground to a halt. Neither of them seemed to know what to say next.

Clearing his throat, Evan claimed his glass.

The faint clink of ice filled the quiet between them. "I didn't know you knew Andrea."

"I didn't know you did. You two seem, um, close."

"I suppose we are," he admitted, taking a sip of the sweetened brew.

"Really?"

"It's not what you think," he went on. "Andrea's my secretary. She works for the department. And we're not dating, if that's what you were thinking. She can be flirty, but that's just the way she is."

Heat crept into Isla's cheeks. Oh. So it was nothing, after all.

"She's not anyone special?"

He chuckled. "No." Leaning back, his gaze sparked. "You're not jealous, are you?"

"Not in the slightest."

"I see. No feelings for me, then? Not even a little?"

Isla swallowed, fighting the flutter in her chest. Admitting she still cared would be like unlocking a floodgate. One that would release a torrent of complications.

"Not the way you think." It was a small lie, but shame had already begun to twist her conscience. She'd plead for divine forgiveness later.

"And that is?"

"Let's just say we've both moved on from whatever we had," she blurted. "I'm not jealous other women might find you attractive. That's only natural. I was just thrown, seeing you two were so friendly."

"Got it," he said. "I'm sorry if Andrea made you feel uncomfortable. She really is just that way. But it doesn't mean anything."

The sincerity in his tone made Isla's heart ache even more. The past couldn't be undone, but she was tired of carrying it.

"It's fine. It just reminded me that things didn't work between us."

Evan leaned forward. "That was my fault." His gaze met hers with a mix of regret and sorrow. "But life goes on, doesn't it?"

"*Ja*, it does."

Silence again. The complexity of their past and the uncertainty of their present was a difficult barrier to overcome. The longer they sat, the more the tension seemed to thicken around them.

Isla sucked in a breath, her fingers nervously fidgeting with the frayed edge of her apron.

"Evan, I'm exhausted from walking on eggshells around our past. Since the day you walked into my *haus*, it feels like we've been stuck in this endless loop, dredging up memories that should have been left behind long ago. We both know it's over and done with. It has been for years."

"I'm aware." With a stiff movement, he started to rise. "I should probably go."

Shaking her head, Isla waved her hands. "Sit down. I'm not finished."

He sank back. "Okay…" The single word was muted as if he wasn't sure he was ready to hear what she might say next.

"Listen to me," she continued, her voice growing steadier. "I care for you. I always have. And now that we've reconnected, I don't want to lose you from my life."

"Go on."

"We can't go back to how things were when we were young, but I would like for us to be friends again, if that's possible."

He offered a genuine smile, the kind that spoke of a shared desire for a fresh start. "I don't have many. But if you're willing, I'd like that."

The sincerity in his tone melted away the last of the awkwardness hanging between them. They might never bridge the gap that separated their worlds, but the warmth of renewed friendship could offer solace and companionship. Both understood that while their lives had taken different paths, their bond still held the potential for something meaningful.

Relieved the tension had eased, Isla reached for a cookie. Freshly baked, its edges were slightly crisp. "I'll have to get Hazel's recipe." She took another bite. "These are the best I've ever tasted."

"She wanted to send something," he explained. "Thanks again for looking in on her while I was in the hospital."

Isla brushed the crumbs off her fingers. "My pleasure."

"As much as I hate to admit it, Hazel's slowing down. She can't live on her own anymore."

"It's hard to see someone you care about not being as independent as they once were. I'm sure she's grateful to have you nearby."

"It was a tough decision, but it was the right one. She's always been there for me. I couldn't let her struggle alone."

"*Familie* is everything," she replied.

"Not got much of that left," he said behind a grimace. "I guess you heard about my *daed*…"

"Hazel mentioned Jonah and Leah had come to the hospital."

"Oh, they came all right," he said. "I'd just been rolled into the ER and then I find out *Daed* is there having a fine froth."

"I'm sorry to hear that."

"He always did have a temper when emotions were running high. His way or the highway, you know. Guess since I took that road, he isn't ever going to forgive me. He's been against everything I've ever done."

"It must have been difficult to deal with."

"Thankfully, *Mamm* was there to drag him off before it got too bad." He winced again, touching his wounded shoulder. "At least I got to hug her before they knocked me out." Mouth going flat, he tapped his fingers against the table, the rhythmic motion betraying his inner turmoil.

Isla's heart ached. The fleeting moment he'd shared with his mother must have meant the world to him.

"I'm glad you got to see her," she said. Her dearest hope was that Evan might, someday, repair his fractured relationship with his stern *vater*. Everyone who knew Jonah was aware his temper was as fiery as his emotions were intense; those who crossed him found themselves swiftly shut out, left in the cold by the older man's searing displeasure.

"Me, too." His gaze swept across the neatly kept garden that stretched out behind the house.

As if on cue, Joel and Olivia burst through the back gate, their faces flushed. Amish schools let out earlier than the *Englisch* ones, a tradition that marked the start of warmer days. After tending to their chores, the children were free to join other *youngies* in the neighborhood for an afternoon of games.

"Finished playing so soon?" Isla called.

Olivia skipped toward the porch with her usual quiet grace, but Joel stomped along with a scowl.

"Joel?" Isla rose from her chair, concern softening her voice. "What's wrong, *lieb*?"

Joel wiped the back of his hand across his sweaty brow, his face tight with frustration. "The big kids won't let me play baseball."

"That doesn't seem fair. Everyone should be allowed to join in." She knew all too well the challenges her youngest faced. His asthma had left him smaller and frailer than other boys his age. She wanted nothing more than for him to be active, to run and play with the other *kinder*, but time and time again they pushed him aside.

"He can't throw," Olivia blurted. "And he keeps dropping the ball."

Joel's face crumpled, his fingers curling tightly around the hem of his shirt as he fought to hold back tears. "I'm trying hard, but I'm not very *gut*," he whispered, his voice thick with disappointment.

Isla bit her lip. She knew her *sohn* was trying. But no matter how much he pushed himself, he couldn't keep up with the other boys.

"Oh, Joel," she murmured, pulling him into her arms. Both children had struggled since losing their father. Joel especially had taken Owen's passing hard. The sparkle had dimmed in his once-bright eyes, replaced by a quiet sadness. A boy needed his *vater*.

Evan cleared his throat. "Maybe I could help. I played ball back in the day. What if I coached him?"

Joel's eyes, red-rimmed and brimming with uncertainty, flicked up to Evan. "You'd teach me?"

"Absolutely." He glanced toward her. "If you say it's okay."

Moved by the sight of her *sohn*'s hopeful expression, Isla looked from one to the other. Despite her reservations about letting someone new into their lives, she saw the sincerity in Evan's eyes and the genuine offer of support. He needed something to focus on as much as Joel did.

After a moment's hesitation, she answered, her voice soft but firm. "It is."

Joel stood near the makeshift home plate, gripping the bat awkwardly. The boy's thin frame was a stark contrast to the sturdiness of the bat he held, and the light, ragged breaths he took revealed the asthma that had kept him from more vigorous play in the past.

Olivia stood at first base. She was a natural athlete, her movements fluid and graceful as she bounced on the balls of her feet, ready to help. Punching the worn leather mitt on her hand, her eyes sparkled with enthusiasm.

"Okay, Joel, let's start with your stance," Evan said, crouching down to the boy's level. "Remember, you want to hold the bat up high and keep your elbows bent."

Joel adjusted his grip, the bat trembling slightly in his small hands. "I got it."

Olivia gave an encouraging smile from her spot. "You've got this," she called out.

Evan took a step back, observing the boy with a critical but kind eye. "Now, I'm going to toss the ball underhand, nice and slow. Just try to swing when you see the ball coming."

"Okay!" Joel squeaked.

The ball sailed through the air.

Joel swung with all his might. The bat met the ball with a satisfying thwack, and it soared in the air before hitting the ground.

The youngster's face lit up with a triumphant grin. "I did it!"

"You sure did," Evan said. "Not bad. Let's see if you can do it again."

Olivia stepped in to retrieve the ball. "That was *gut*."

"Keep your eye on the ball and follow through with your swing," Evan added.

The practice continued.

As the afternoon wore on, Evan pitched ball after ball. And though his injured arm gave him a few twinges, he worked through the discomfort by focusing on the game. Joel swung with increasing confidence. Despite the occasional wheeze from his asthma, his determination never wavered.

Evan saw the joy in Joel's eyes and the pride in Olivia's face as they worked together. The sense of camaraderie was palpable, and he found himself drawn into the simple pleasure of the game. The sound of laughter and the occasional playful argument over the rules filled the air, creating a sense of warmth and belonging that he hadn't experienced in a long time.

All in all, it was an enjoyable experience.

As the sun began its descent, Isla appeared at the edge of the yard, her apron dusted with flour. She waved to catch their attention. "Supper's almost ready. Would you care to join us?"

He hesitated. Spending more time with Isla and her kids was appealing, but he had obligations. "I would like to, but I've got to get back home. I'm sure Hazel is wondering what happened to me."

"I understand," Isla said. "Please thank her for all the goodies she sent."

"I'll be sure and pass it along." He lingered, his boots scuffing against the ground, reluctant to leave. The opportunity to indulge in a simple pleasure had done wonders to lift his spirits.

"Could you come back and play again?" Joel's small voice broke through his thoughts. Expression hopeful, his wide eyes were bright and innocent.

"Sometime soon?" Olivia chimed in.

"It's really up to your *mamm*," he said.

Isla's lips curved, her eyes meeting his with warmth. "Sometime would be nice." There was a softness in her voice, but beneath it lay a hint of distance. She wasn't making any promises. "Now go. I know Hazel is waiting."

Leaving brought a pang of longing. The afternoon had been a glimpse into a life he'd often wondered about. A life with people he loved, with laughter and shared moments. It was a stark contrast to his solitary existence, marked by the quiet of his old lifestyle and the responsibilities that weighed on him.

"I'll be in touch," he said, a promise he wasn't sure how he'd keep but one he needed to make.

"We'll be here."

Walking to his truck, Evan glanced back one last time, catching sight of Joel and Olivia waving at him from the front stoop. The scene was a heartwarming snapshot. He sighed as he settled behind the wheel, the reality of being a single man pressing back in.

The drive home wasn't as pleasant. The radio played on, but each song seemed to underscore his loneliness, with their melodies drenched in themes of single men, long nights and the familiar solace of drinking alone. The tunes drifted through the airwaves, their lyrics echoing his own solitude.

Fiddling with the dials, he tried to find something more uplifting, but every country song seemed to mirror his inner turmoil. The music amplified the emptiness of his life.

Pulling into the driveway, he set his hands on the steering wheel and took a few deep breaths. *You need to get a grip on this.*

Dwelling in sadness and regret wasn't any way

to face the future. He needed to focus on what lay ahead, confronting the challenges with resolve.

As he pushed open the front door, the sight that greeted him was unexpectedly calming. The old farmhouse, with its creaky wooden floors and spacious charm, radiated a tranquil atmosphere. The faded floral wallpaper and hand-stitched quilts draped over the furniture created a comforting, old-fashioned ambiance.

Hazel sat in her favorite armchair, working on her knitting; Hambone was snuggled up on a dog bed nearby, snoring gently. Nearby, Stewart was industriously rummaging through her yarns. The once-tidy basket was a chaotic mess of reds, blues and greens, which the raccoon seemed to find utterly fascinating.

"You've been gone a while," she remarked, pushing her spectacles up the bridge of her nose. "I was starting to get worried."

Evan hung his worn Stetson on the brass hook by the door. "You've got a cell phone now. You could've called."

Hazel waved a hand, brushing off the suggestion. "Oh, that thing? You know I'm not one for intruding."

"That's the whole point of it," he said. "I want you to stay in touch. Anything could happen. You need to be able to reach out in an emergency."

"I didn't want to be a bother." A familiar hint of defiance laced her tone.

"Well, it's there if you need it." His aunt had always been as tough as an old hickory tree, and just as unyielding. In all his years, he had never seen anyone dig their heels in quite like her. "When I'm not here, you know how to contact me."

Hazel waved him off with a huff. "Where have you been, anyway? A trip to the hardware store shouldn't have taken all day." Her gaze narrowed, making it clear she wouldn't accept excuses. "I hope you didn't shrug off my errand."

"I went by Isla's, just like you asked." He ran a hand through his disheveled hair as he sank into an armchair by the window. "Spent most of the afternoon there, if you want to know." The truth was, the hardware store had slipped his mind, a casualty of his preoccupation with the day's unexpected pleasures.

The old lady's face brightened. "Oh? Do tell."

"We had a nice visit," he said. "I ended up playing ball with her kids for a couple of hours. Oh, I forgot to say she sends her thanks for the extras."

"It's *gut* to see you getting out and spending time with friends." Hazel resumed her knitting, her needles clicking rhythmically as she worked.

Evan stared down at the floor, tapping the toe of his boot against the scuffed wooden floor. "Do you think it would be okay to see her again?"

Hazel didn't look up. "Is that what you want?"

"Yeah, I do," he said. "But would it be proper?

I mean, well, I wouldn't want anyone to get any ideas about my intentions."

His concern was genuine; he wanted to be mindful of boundaries and respect the memory of Isla's late husband. He knew that his visits might be interpreted in various ways, and the last thing he wanted was to cause any misunderstandings or unintended gossip. The Amish community had always been tolerant of *Englischer*s, but he also knew there were unspoken rules and subtle nuances in their interactions. Certain social lines could never be crossed.

"Which would be?"

He faltered. "I'm not sure."

Hazel tilted her head slightly, her expression softening. "The old spark is still there, isn't it?"

"If that means do I still have feelings for Isla, then yes. I guess I do." The admission felt heavy, ladened with years of unresolved emotions. It felt too soon. Too complicated. But he also couldn't deny the truth any longer.

"Is it something you think you'd like to follow up on?"

"I think so, but it wouldn't be simple." He paused, then released a long breath, feeling the enormity of what he was considering. "If I were to pursue something with Isla, I'd have to change everything. My life, my job, my standing with the Amish community." Basically, he'd be starting from scratch.

"I'm glad you're thinking about it," she said, needles clicking softly as she worked. "I was wondering when you'd finally reach this point."

"What do you mean?"

"You're of an age when it's time to start thinking about what you want for the future, not just in terms of your job, but in terms of your personal life."

Relief swept over him, a surprising wave that he hadn't expected. He hadn't realized how desperately he needed someone to acknowledge what had been swirling in his mind for months.

"You're right," he allowed. "That's exactly what I've been thinking about."

"Maybe *Gott*'s been trying to tell you this all along. You've just been too busy to listen."

Evan stared at the floor. He wasn't one to easily share his feelings, especially about matters of the heart. But this felt different. The idea of making such a drastic change was terrifying. And yet, there was a part of him that felt drawn to it, as if he was being pulled in a direction he hadn't yet allowed himself to explore.

"I never thought about it like that." The words were hard to say, the vulnerability unfamiliar and uncomfortable. But it was the truth. He had been so caught up in his job, in the chaos of life, that he hadn't stopped to consider that maybe, just maybe, there was something more waiting for him. Something better.

"I think it would help if you spent time among your own again," she advised. "Reconnect with the people who knew you before all this. Get to know them, and yourself, again."

Chapter Seven

The late afternoon sun cast long shadows across the rows of wooden tables adorned with hand-sewn quilts, homemade baskets and other Amish crafts and goods. A light breeze carried the mouthwatering aromas of fresh-baked desserts mingling with the hum of laughter and conversation as families gathered for the charity event.

This year, the cause held special significance. The *Boppli* Bank, a cherished community initiative designed to aid struggling mothers, was raising funds for a new and vital project: a Safe Haven Baby Box. Sponsored by the church, the charity event served as a rare and meaningful opportunity for both Amish and *Englischer*s to come together for a common purpose. The box would be installed at the local volunteer fire station, offering a secure and anonymous way for desperate mothers to surrender their newborns without fear of judgment or prosecution. For many in the community, especially those who had once faced their own silent battles, the project struck a tender chord.

The gathering offered not just good food, but a lively array of games, activities and fellowship, drawing in people of all ages to support the project. It was more than just a fundraiser. It was a celebration of giving, where every smile, every warm greeting and every dollar raised would help make a difference.

As an active supporter of local charities, it wasn't unusual for Evan to attend on behalf of the sheriff's department. His presence would also help reassure the townsfolk that he was on the mend.

Moving through the crowd, his gaze swept through the gathering, pausing on familiar faces. Among them were the Schroder sisters, all four gathered with their husbands and children.

The sight of the women stopped him in his tracks. He hadn't realized how much time had passed since he'd last seen them all together. He'd stood at the edges of their lives, watching them mature and change. No longer the girls he'd grown up with, they'd all become wives and mothers.

Gail's cheerful laugh cut through the hum of the gathering as she tried to wrangle her boisterous brood. Rebecca stood nearby, her calm presence a stark contrast to Gail's lively energy. She eagerly shared news about her youngest, yet another foster fail. So far, they'd adopted three orphaned *Englisch* children. Then there was Amity, chasing after energetic twin toddlers as they darted around the park. And Florene...well, Florene was radiant. It was strange to see her back in the community after all these years, stranger still to see her as a mother. Married to Gilead Kestler, she had two boys now, and the love she had for them shone in every smile she gave them, every gentle touch.

Remembering Florene's trauma with her ex-boyfriend, he wondered what it had taken for her to return to the Amish, what scars she carried beneath the surface. He understood the weight of the past better than most, after all. He'd always felt like he was on the periphery of this world, part of it, but not fully immersed. Maybe that's why he'd never settled down, why he'd drifted—searching, but never quite finding a place to land.

If only he'd chosen differently, how might his life have unfolded? It was a question with no answer. The door to the past had closed long ago. But the future now stretched before him, offering a new path, another chance. All that remained was the choice. Whether to walk away and let it be or to take the turn in the road and see where it might lead.

Pleased as he was to see everyone, the one person he'd most wanted to visit with was missing. As far as he could tell, Isla wasn't in attendance. He'd imagined what it would be like; the way their eyes might meet, how her smile might warm the ache that had been sitting in his chest for days.

The hope he'd been holding onto began to fade, a slow, heavy sinking feeling settling in its place.

It's not as if we're seeing each other.

An involuntary chill spread through him, betraying the casualness he tried to maintain. He gave himself a swift mental kick, frustrated by the emotions that surfaced whenever he thought about her. There was no reason to get carried away—they weren't anything more than friends, after all. But the way her smile lingered in his mind long after she left made it hard to believe that.

Suddenly, he didn't want to be there.

Surrounded by laughter and casual conversation, he'd never felt more isolated. Everyone seemed to be part of something. Spouses exchanging knowing glances, children tugging at their parents' sleeves. He was the odd one out, the only one without a family to anchor him. The feeling of not belonging, of drifting on the outskirts of their contentment, made the air around him seem thicker, harder to breathe.

"Well, look at you," a familiar voice called.

Evan glanced up to see Levi Wyse sauntering over with a grin. He was accompanied by two of his brothers-in-law, Ethan Zehr and Caleb Sutter. Together, they formed a protective unit, bound not just by marriage, but by an unspoken understanding of loyalty and shared responsibility.

"*Gut* to see you're back on your feet," Levi said, offering his hand.

Evan returned a firm shake, though the twinge in his arm reminded him healing wasn't done. "Got back up as soon as I could." The perp had been aiming to put him six feet under, but here he was, alive and doing his best to shake off his injury like it was nothing more than a minor scrape.

"How's the shoulder?" A skilled physician, Caleb had chosen to settle in the Amish community after a life-altering revelation. Put up for adoption in the *Englisch* world, he'd later learned his mother was Amish—young, pregnant and unwed, she'd attempted to hide her shame by leaving her community. His return had been met with acceptance, allowing him to bridge the gap between the two worlds with his medical expertise. He wore the traditional beard of a married Amish man, but it was neatly trimmed—a compromise between professional standards and the customs of his faith.

Evan flexed his hand. "Almost good as new."

"You probably don't remember," Caleb continued, "but I did your triage when you came through the ER. You had me a little worried."

"Truth is, I don't."

That day, everything had merged into a blur of shock and pain, the edges softened by the haze of disbelief. The initial jolt of the bullet striking vulnerable flesh had been a sharp, white-hot stab that seemed to freeze time itself. Realizing he'd been struck, a crushing wave of confusion and helplessness had overwhelmed him, swallowing his senses in a suffocating grip. He could barely piece together the fragments of what had happened next, each recollection slipping through his fingers like sand, leaving him with nothing but a gnawing emptiness where clarity should have been.

"I have to admit, I couldn't handle your job," Ethan Zehr said, his voice laden with genuine admiration. "It takes a kind of bravery that I can barely imagine."

"I don't know if I'd call it that, but thank you."

"I want you to know how much it means to all of us that you're still here," Levi said. "We've all had to call on you at one time or another, and we're grateful for everything you did for the *familie*."

"Just doing my job." Helping people, righting the wrongs that life threw at them, was why he'd joined law enforcement in the first place.

"Any chance you know what's going on with that fella who did it?" Ethan asked. "The robberies have a lot of people spooked, but this has really got them on edge. Amity has insisted that we put cameras and alarms in the *kaffeeshop*." Shaking his head, he added, "Never thought I'd agree, but I do."

"I've not received any updates," Evan confessed, determined to be as transparent as possible. "There was evidence at the scene and that'll be processed. If any viable DNA is recovered, we might have a chance of identifying him."

Levi rocked back on his heels, a thoughtful expression on his face. "I hear the Texas Rangers have stepped in."

"That's right. They've got a reputation for getting results where others fall short. If anyone can track down this guy, it's them."

Levi chuckled, clearly impressed. "They don't mess around, do they?"

"No, they don't. I'm confident they'll crack the case."

"What about you?" Ethan asked. "Any chance you're going to get in on it?"

"I'm hopeful," Evan replied. "But I'm on medical leave. Until I'm told differently, that's where I'll stay."

"I'm aware of the protocols," Caleb said. "Can't say I don't agree with them. A shooting is a traumatic event for anyone."

"I'm not happy about being sidelined, but it's part of the process." His appointment with the psychiatrist was still in limbo. All he could do was wait it out and hope for the best.

The small talk continued among the men. Conversation thankfully moved on, touching on the usual subjects farmers and ranchers were inclined to be interested in—the weather, crops and live-stock.

Acutely aware he knew little to nothing about such things, Evan listened with half an ear. Each burst of laughter and nod of agreement from the other men seemed to push him away. It occurred to him that while he knew these people, he didn't really fit in with the group.

Feeling isolated, he bid the men good day and moved on. His own relatives were in attendance, but there was no point in approaching them; his *daed* remained distant, his *mamm* offered only a fleeting smile. His younger brothers—David, James and Matthias—waved briefly before turning away. Jonah Miller had made it clear that he had no place in the family, and that was the end of it.

Sighing, he wandered around looking for familiar faces. A few staffers from his office were in attendance.

Dressed in a chic ensemble, Andrea Richards browsed the variety of selections at a vendor's table. "Hi there!" she called out.

"Fancy meeting you here," he greeted.

"Oh, I wouldn't dream of missing this," she replied, her enthusiasm just slightly overplayed. "I find the Amish so quaint. They are lovely people, really. And of course, it's always nice to support a worthy cause, don't you think?"

"It's more than just a charity," he said. "It's

a chance to make a real difference locally. I'm happy to give what I can to make sure we keep helping those in need."

"I didn't get a chance to call you earlier," Andrea said, shifting the conversation slightly, "but I need you to come by the office when you have a moment."

"Oh? What about?"

"HR sent down some insurance paperwork," she replied. "A few things need your signature."

"I'll come in on Monday."

"Thanks."

"How are things at the office?"

Andrea gave a slight shrug. "Busy. We're stretched thin right now, but we're managing."

"I'm sure Lopez is doing fine," he said, his hands instinctively curling into fists before relaxing again. "Any updates on the thief?"

Andrea's posture stiffened slightly. Her eyes flickered toward him, and her tone turned cautious. "You know I can't discuss internal matters with someone on administrative leave, Sheriff."

"Right," he muttered, his jaw tightening. "Of course."

The weight of being sidelined from the investigation bore down on him, a troubling sense of isolation threading through his thoughts. It was the same old feeling, that haunting sense of being on the outside, looking in.

The longer he stayed out of the game, the more irrelevant he became. And the more isolated.

"Come on, Joel, pedal faster!" Olivia urged, glancing back at her younger brother.

Face scrunched, Joel's brows were knitted tightly as he fought against the resistance of the pedals. Sweat glistened on his forehead, mixing with the dust of the road that clung to his cheeks. His hands gripped the handlebars with tenacity, his breath coming in ragged bursts that matched the frantic rhythm of his pedaling.

"We're not in any rush," Isla called out, her voice soothing yet firm as she rode slightly behind the two, her eyes darting between the road and her children. "We'll get there when we get there."

Before Owen's passing, the idea of riding a bike had never crossed her mind. She'd always taken for granted the steady comfort of their horse and buggy. But after his death, their world had changed. Selling the buggy to make ends meet had been a sensible decision at the time, but now, every bump in the road was a reminder of what they had lost. Sometimes neighbors offered rides, but she hated imposing too often. Independence meant something different now. At least the bicycles gave them some mobility, however limited and awkward.

You could have declined the invitation to participate.

But she hadn't said no. A chance to break the monotony of her daily routine and socialize sounded fun.

The possibility of seeing Evan also crossed her mind. She'd caught glimpses of him at many such gatherings in the past. Despite this, their interactions had always been minimal. A polite nod here, a fleeting smile there. To respect Owen's feelings, she'd made a conscious effort not to show any traces of familiarity with the lawman. Given their tangled past, it was simpler to maintain a distance.

Now things were different. As she approached the end of her year of mourning, the expectations on her were shifting. The *Leit* would expect her to reenter social life. At her age, remarrying was considered not only desirable, but necessary.

The fact that Evan was still single hadn't escaped her notice. Neither had the fact that as former Amish, he still had the option of rejoining the brethren. It wasn't uncommon for those who had left to return to their roots, seeking solace in the familiar ways of their upbringing.

Since they'd started speaking again, a part of her couldn't help but wonder if he might find something in their close-knit community that would finally tempt him to leave behind the harsh, dangerous world of law enforcement.

The flickering hope seemed fragile, almost foolish. Still, she held it close. *Gott* promised to restore what was lost, after all. The Bible spoke of mercy, of His compassion for those who sought His grace.

The blaring of a car horn yanked her from her thoughts, the sound sharp and jarring. Before she could react, a silvery car whipped past, close enough that she felt the rush of air trailing behind it. Speeding down the road, it disappeared into the distance before she fully registered what had occurred.

Frightened by the close call, Joel wobbled dangerously, but somehow managed to keep his balance. Beside him, Olivia's face had gone pale, her wide eyes tracking the receding car and her mouth open in surprise.

Isla's pulse thudded as she took a steadying breath. "Stay closer to the curb," she warned. Always in a hurry, *Englisch* drivers were so careless.

Thankfully, the park's pavilion came into view, a welcoming beacon of celebration and camaraderie. Familiar figures were already gathered, their laughter and voices indicating a lively get-together.

Following the path to the parking lot, Isla guided the children to a spot where they could safely dismount. Joel and Olivia were quick to hop off, their faces flushed but excited.

Olivia's expression brightened. "There's Cassidy and Cathy!" she exclaimed, pointing toward Rebecca and Caleb Sutter's adopted daughters. The couple had initially taken in the older girl and her sibling as fosters, but their bond had grown so strong that fostering had quickly turned into a permanent arrangement. They'd also adopted a third *youngie* and wanted more.

Joel's eyes lit up as he noticed a group of older boys playing catch with a Frisbee. "Do you think they'd let me play?" he asked, his voice full of excitement and hope.

Isla propped her bike on its stand. "I'm sure they would." Now grown and well beyond their school years, Liam Zehr and Seth Wyse had become exemplary young men. Their kindness and maturity shone through in everything they did. Active in the church youth group, they not only contributed their time but also mentored younger *boi*s who were struggling, guiding them away from trouble and toward a better path.

Both children ran ahead, greeting their friends and joining in on the games.

Isla lingered behind, scanning the array of faces around her. Her pulse skipped a beat when she finally spotted Evan. Excitement faltered when she noticed that he wasn't alone. Andrea Richards stood close by, her presence commanding his attention. The two appeared to be deep in conversation, a stark contrast to the rest of the gathering's relaxed mingling.

Ach, *that woman!* What was she doing here? It wasn't that she disliked the *Englischer.* Andrea was a customer who paid well. But there was something about the other woman's overly familiar demeanor that rubbed her the wrong way.

Unsettled by the sight, Isla turned to the basket on her bicycle. She'd prepared a loaf of her signature cinnamon-pecan monkey bread. Easy to wrap and transport, it was one of her most beloved recipes.

"Isla!" Rebecca Sutter called, her face lighting up with a welcoming smile. "You made it!" A beacon of kindness, Rebecca was known for dedication that extended far beyond personal gestures. After helping Caleb care for an abandoned infant, she'd founded the *Boppli* Bank to help young mothers in need.

"I'm so glad you came!" she continued, enveloping Isla in a quick but heartfelt hug.

Gail Wyse and Amity Zehr also greeted her, their faces glowing with friendly warmth.

"We'd wondered what happened," Gail exclaimed.

"I was about to send Ethan and Liam to look for you," Amity added.

"We had trouble with the bicycles," Isla explained, placing her dish among the other offerings on the table. "But we're here now."

"You are okay?" Amity asked. "We heard about the break-in at your shop."

Isla momentarily faltered. The memories still haunted her. The sight of her disheveled *haus* was something she'd never forget.

"The Lord got us through," she answered, determined to move past the incident. "All I lost was a little money. That can be replaced."

Gail's eyes softened with concern. "Still, it must have been so scary."

"Not nearly as much as what happened afterward—" Her words faltered as a lump formed in her throat. The memory of Evan in that sterile hospital room, unconscious and injured, gripped with a relentless squeeze. At the same time, her mind raced back to the frightening thought: What if she'd arrived home ten minutes earlier that fateful afternoon? The chilling notion that she, or one of her *kinder*, might have been injured, too, made her blood run cold.

Rebecca leaned closer. She gave a subtle nod toward Hazel, who sat nearby chatting with friends.

"We're not going to talk about that right now," she whispered, her gaze flickering with a mix of concern and resolve. "Not with Hazel right over there."

"I heard about her fall, but you know how stubborn she is," Gail said. "Never one to admit she needs help. I'm glad Evan's there for her. He's always been someone you could count on."

Amity also glanced in the old woman's direction, a thoughtful expression on her face. "At least he has an *amisches familienmitglied* who still shows him kindness. I could be wrong, but it seems like they need each other, you know?"

"It bothers me how the Millers have treated both of them," Rebecca added behind her hand. "I may sit in the same church with Jonah, but I can't say I approve of his behavior. It's as if he's forgotten the very principles we hold dear."

Thankfully the conversation took a turn toward a more cheerful subject and Isla threw herself into the lively hustle of the bake sale. She busied herself behind one of the tables, her hands moving deftly as she counted coins and crumpled bills with practiced ease. The soft hum of chatter filled the air, punctuated by the clinking of change and the occasional burst of laughter.

Browsers meandered by, their eyes lighting up at the array of homemade treats. Amish bakers had offered a feast for the senses, creating a variety of cakes, cookies and delicious pies. *Englischer*s admired the displays, exchanging appreciative comments about the tantalizing dishes.

"Hey, stranger," a voice greeted her from behind. "Fancy seeing you here."

Isla involuntarily tensed at the unexpected encounter. Seeing Andrea with Evan, she'd hoped not to run into the woman. The last thing she wanted was a drawn-out conversation with a female whose presence seemed to amplify the unsettled feeling in her chest.

Shaking off her dismay, she forced a smile that she hoped was more genuine than it felt. "It's nice to see you again, Miss Richards."

Andrea gave a casual wave, her well-manicured hand fluttering in the air. "Now don't start that nonsense. Please, call me Andrea." Shaking a finger, she added, "We are friends."

Isla managed a faint, polite smile. No, they were just acquaintances. Nothing more.

"Is there something I can assist you with?" she asked, striving to keep her voice even.

Andrea's gaze drifted over the array of desserts. "I was looking for something to drink. I've only found water and sodas for sale. I sure could use something a little stronger."

"The Amish don't serve or consume alcohol," Isla said. "It's not in keeping with our traditions."

Andrea let out a small, resigned chuckle, her smile faltering. "Right. That makes sense. I guess it's for the best, especially considering how some folks here have had their share of struggles with, um, moderation."

Isla bristled. "Is that so?"

"Oh, you'd be surprised," Andrea said, her voice carrying an air of casual confidence, as if she were sharing an open secret. "Amish teens get picked up more often than you'd think. Nothing serious, though. The sheriff usually just sends them home with a warning." She leaned in slightly, as if she were about to disclose something more personal. "Not to spread gossip, you understand, but even Miller has been known to stroll into the office looking rough around the edges, if you catch my meaning."

"Really?"

Andrea waved her hands dismissively, a casual smile playing on her lips. "Not that it's any of my business. No judgment here."

Isla forced a smile, but inside, her thoughts swirled. Andrea did work in the sheriff's department. If anyone had insight into Evan's daily routine, it would be her.

But was it the truth, or an exaggeration? Small-town gossip often grew as the stories went around. But now, hearing Andrea speak with such certainty, she wasn't so sure.

Recalling her last visit with Evan, a knot of worry coiled tight in Isla's chest. He'd seemed well enough, laughing and playing ball with Joel and Olivia for most of the afternoon. But there were fleeting moments when his expression had clouded, as if something unsettling lurked just beneath the surface of his thoughts.

At the time, she'd dismissed it as the aftereffects of his injury, the frustration of being placed on leave. But now she wondered if it went deeper.

Was there something far more troubling gnawing at him?

Chapter Eight

Time slipped away, its steady march unbroken. Days vanished before Evan even realized they'd passed.

Seeking refuge from anxiety, he found a quiet sense of satisfaction in the routine he'd created for himself. The old farmhouse, once sturdy but now creaking under its accumulated years, was in constant need of repairs. There was always something to fix—leaky faucets, drafty windows, rotting floorboards. Each repair he completed brought a quiet sense of pride. He took satisfaction in the skills he was slowly, steadily mastering.

Despite his best efforts to stay busy, the emptiness inside him remained. No matter how many nails he hammered or windows he sealed, the void lingered. He hadn't seen Isla since the charity event. She'd been there, bustling behind the bake sale table, her hands busy and her smile warm and effortless. He'd watched her from a distance, unsure, his feet anchored by hesitation. He couldn't bring himself to interrupt, even though he'd craved spending time with her. Every chance to speak had eluded him, lost in the flow of people and the flurry of activity.

He'd told himself it didn't matter. But the days had rolled on, unyielding, and *another time* never seemed to come. The ache of missed opportunity grew heavier with each passing day.

And then, he crumbled.

The anniversary he always dreaded loomed, an unwanted reminder of what had been lost. Dreadful memories surged, pulling him back to that fateful day: Echoes of laughter twisted into screams, the joys of a sunny afternoon replaced by the grip of tragedy…

Evan stood before the grave, the weight of years pressing down on him as he gazed at the modest headstone. Save for the distant murmur of the breeze, the graveyard was quiet. The inscription on the headstone read Lila Mary Miller. Beneath it was the date of her birth and death. Aside from those few simple lines, the stone was blank, devoid of decoration. A small bouquet of roses lay beside the stone. Petals withered, a note was tucked inside the brittle stems.

Believing the flowers to be a thoughtful gesture from a friend or family member, he knelt, carefully tugging the small card from its place.

The dead never rest, it read. *Neither will you.*

A chill traced down his spine, prickling the hairs on the back of his neck. Who would leave such a cruel message? And why?

Senses alert, Evan's gaze swept the cemetery, taking in the weathered headstones. Something felt off, but he couldn't quite place it. Whoever had written the message had left no trace of themselves behind.

Clenching the note tightly, he stuffed it into his pocket, the sharp twist in his chest as fierce as it had been on the day they buried Lila. The passage of time hadn't dulled the ache.

He recoiled as images from that fateful day flashed through his mind. The sound of the truck's engine was forever embedded in his memory. He could never erase the shattering impact, the cries of terror as the nightmare scene replayed in his mind. He remembered the horse's anguished whinny before it fell.

Thrown clear of the wreckage, he'd somehow managed to rise, scrambling to find his younger sister in the chaos of the moment. Lila…oh, Lila… She'd lain on the ground, her eyes half-open, staring blankly at the sky.

Evan closed his eyes, the image of his sister's last moments on earth haunting him. He'd always been the protector, the older brother who took care of the younger ones. Yet he'd failed when she needed him most.

"I'm sorry," he whispered, his voice breaking

under the weight of his grief. "I should have been able to help you."

Lost in the haze of regret, he barely registered the faint crunch of wheels over gravel as a buggy rolled to a stop outside the cemetery gates. The world around him felt distant, muted by the shadow of everything he couldn't change.

A few minutes later, a voice spoke from behind. "Evan?"

Startled, he jerked up from his crouched position, instinctively adopting a defensive stance. His heart pounded, ready for anything except for the sight that met him. Isla stood quietly, her presence as calm and unassuming as the whisper of a breeze.

"What are you doing here?"

"I come every year," she said, stepping closer with a sympathetic smile. "Abner loaned me his buggy for the afternoon." Dressed in solemn black, her long skirts flowed around her slender frame. A black *kapp* framed her face, casting a gentle shadow that highlighted her delicate features. Her long cloak enveloped her in a dignified aura. Every aspect of her attire spoke of a deep, respectful sorrow, mirroring the somber surroundings.

"It's sad to lose someone so young," she continued, her gaze drifting to the gravestone. "I still miss her more than words can say."

"It doesn't seem right she's not here."

"None of us can change the past," she said. "We do what we can, but sometimes it's not enough. Lila wouldn't want you to live in grief."

"I know she wouldn't. But it's hard. Every time I think I'm moving on, something reminds me of her."

"Sometimes, the best way to honor someone's memory is to live your own life fully."

"I haven't found that easy to do." He scrubbed his temple with anxious fingers, letting out a heavy sigh. A dull ache pulsed behind his eyes. Despite his mandatory appointments with the department's psychiatrist, a lot of trauma continued to linger.

Isla's calm demeanor wavered. "It's not. But we have to try." Turning her head, she glanced across the cemetery toward a grassy knoll. "Would you care to visit Owen?"

"Yeah. I think I would."

They walked together, their path leading to a quieter, more secluded section located beneath a spread of trees.

Isla led the way to a modest grave marked by a plain stone. It was unassuming, but there was a certain dignity to its simplicity.

As they drew nearer, Evan felt a pang of sorrow for his childhood friend. The news of Owen's illness and his abrupt passing had rocked everyone who knew him. It was a heart-wrenching blow. A vibrant young man, gone far too soon.

Once again, the fragility of life slammed into him with brutal force. Survival was a borrowed gift, one he didn't deserve.

"I can't believe Owen's gone. So young, too. Doesn't seem like he got to live."

Isla dabbed at her eyes with a handkerchief. "I have happy memories of him. He gave me a *gut* life and two fine *kinder*."

"Joel and Olivia are incredible kids. I know Owen would be proud of them for holding up the way they have."

"*Ja*. It was hard on both. But they are learning to understand that *Gott* gives each of us our years. All we can do is make the best of the time we're given, try to leave a mark of goodness before He calls us home."

The significance of her words pressed on Evan. Talking about the Lord always stirred something inside him, something raw and jagged. It wasn't just discomfort; it was a gnawing unease. How could he speak of faith when his own relationship with God felt so fractured?

He glanced at Isla, her grief evident in the tremble of her shoulders. Giving her a gentle nudge, he indicated the nearby bench, shaded by an old oak tree.

"Let's sit for a minute."

Isla nodded, tucking her handkerchief into her apron pocket. They walked together in near silence, the quiet rustle of leaves dancing in the gentle breeze, wrapping around them.

As they settled onto the bench, the air felt heavy. The cryptic message on Lila's grave continued to gnaw at him, refusing to be forgotten. It felt as if the dead weren't the only ones left without peace. The living carried their burdens, too,

"I'm glad to see you," he finally said, his voice a bit strained. "I meant to stop by, but I didn't want to be a bother."

"Joel was hoping you'd want to come and play ball again sometime. Olivia, too."

"I wanted to, but I didn't want to make it seem like I was butting in or anything like that."

A soft smile tugged at her lips, illuminating her features. Her fingers entwined nervously in her lap as if they were unsure of their purpose. "I think it's *gut* for them," she replied. "It shows them that our lives move on and that it's all right to be happy again."

"What about you? Are you happy?"

"I'm content," she answered softly. "Even after all that's happened, I still have so much to be thankful for. I have my *youngies*. And we have a roof over our heads and food in our bellies. And *Gott* gave me two *gut* hands to make a living. We might not have everything we want, but we have what we need. I'm grateful the Lord has blessed us."

Her gaze drifted to the sky. The serenity in her

expression mirrored the peacefulness of the setting, as if she was drawing strength from the simplicity around her. Her humility made her even more admirable. She was a woman who, even when life pressed her, sought out the good in each day and prayed away the bad.

For a moment silence stretched between them, heavy but not uncomfortable.

"Are you happy?" she asked.

Evan's first instinct was to shrug it off with a casual "I'm fine." But she wasn't asking out of politeness; she truly wanted to know.

"I don't think I've been happy in a long time," he admitted. The burden of his past was a millstone, dragging him down with its crushing gravity. The walls he'd built around himself kept others from getting too close. Untouched and untouchable, he'd made a lot of mistakes. Mistakes he dearly regretted.

"What do you think is missing?"

He didn't answer right away. He'd spent years avoiding the question. But here, with Isla beside him, the truth felt inevitable.

"God," he said finally. "He's not in my life. Not the way He should be."

Isla's face softened with understanding, her eyes reflecting compassion rather than judgment. "The Lord's always there," she said gently. "Even when you feel far away, He's still waiting for you to come back."

"I'm not sure I believe that," he admitted. "I don't view, uh, religion the way I used to."

Isla's fingers brushed lightly against his arm, her touch grounding him in a way he hadn't expected. "Walking the Lord's path is never easy. We all struggle with it. But sometimes reconnecting with what we've lost can help us find the way forward. Have you thought about coming back to the church? I'm not saying it'll fix everything, but it might be the first step toward healing, toward finding peace."

"I'm the one who turned away," he said. "How could I face the congregation? How could I face God?"

"The Lord hasn't turned His back on you," she said. "Opening your heart to Him won't make everything perfect, but it could help fill that emptiness you feel. It could help you find what's been missing."

Her reassurance touched something deep within him. A part of him wanted to believe her, wanted to reach out for the solace she was offering. But after years of hiding behind alcohol and isolation, he didn't know if he had the strength to take that first step.

"I haven't felt anything in so long."

"It takes time," she said softly. "You don't have to have all the answers right away. Just take the first step. The rest will follow."

He sighed, conflict raging inside him. For so

long, he'd found solace in the bottle, using it to numb his restless mind. Now that he'd discarded that crutch, he was finding it difficult to walk on his own. He was tired of being tired, tired of being lonely. Of being alone. Deep down, he yearned for a life filled with light and laughter, for the warmth that only the presence of loved ones could provide.

"You really believe there's a place for me?"

"*Ja*. I do. And I think you do, too."

For the first time in years, the solution didn't feel so unattainable. Though his past pressed heavily on his shoulders, he sensed a crack in the armor he had built around himself.

If you keep doing nothing, you'll go nowhere.

What did he have to lose? Standing at a crossroads, he realized that his next steps would shape the direction of his journey through life. He could cling to the misery that had become all too familiar or summon the fortitude to step toward a brighter future.

Resistance crumbling, Evan swallowed hard. "I'll be at church Sunday morning."

"Joel! Olivia! It's time to go!"

Joel shuffled down the stairs, dressed in his best clothes. He'd attempted to tame his hair, but a defiant cowlick stood at attention. Olivia followed, her *kapp* strings dancing as she fidgeted with excitement.

Isla hurried both toward the front door. "We mustn't keep the Pilchers waiting."

The trio hurried outside, where the crisp morning air greeted them. Buggy parked at the curb, Abner Pilcher waited to pick them up. Verna sat primly beside him with a basket in hand.

"Running a little late today?" Abner called, chuckling.

"I forgot to wind the alarm clock," she replied as she bundled the children into the cab. What she didn't mention was the extra time she had spent on her personal care: arranging her hair, ironing her dress and polishing her black boots until they shone. She'd even pinched her cheeks, hoping to coax a bit of color back into her pale complexion.

"Never had that trouble," Abner chuckled. "Verna won't let me sleep a minute past five."

"Lying abed is wasting time," Verna countered righteously. "The Lord warns us not to be slothful."

The two set to arguing in that way longtime married folks did.

Settling back on the seat, Isla let the gentle clip-clop of the horse soothe her nerves. The street blurred past, but for a moment, she simply breathed. Today felt different, charged, as if something just beyond her reach might finally shift.

She'd invited Evan to church. His younger sister's death had shattered him—left raw edges and grief he carried like a second skin. Isla had seen it in the set of his shoulders, the silence behind his eyes. He bore guilt that didn't belong to him, but no one could tell him otherwise.

His estrangement from his family added another jagged layer, a wound that hadn't closed since the funeral. And then the shooting… It was too much. Too much for anyone.

But she had wounds, too.

Her gaze dropped to her hands, fingers twisting in her lap. The robbery had left more than a mess. The bills kept piling up, and not enough work was coming in. And then there was the loneliness of loss, pressing in on all sides.

Still, she held on to the fragile thread of hope. Maybe today could be a fresh start. For her—and for Evan.

Lord, please help us both, she prayed.

As they approached their destination, Isla took a deep breath, reminding herself to stay calm. The church—a testament to their enduring traditions—came into view, its whitewashed walls glowing with a timeless purity. A gravel path crunched softly beneath the sturdy boots of the arriving congregation, guiding them toward the heart of their community.

For many, the building was more than just a place of worship; it was a practical answer to the logistical challenges posed by rural living. In the early days, services had been held in the homes of various families. But as the community grew and properties stretched farther apart, this arrangement had become increasingly unwieldy. The journey to different homes each week became too taxing, leading to the establishment of a dedicated location. This central haven provided a common ground where they could gather with ease, bridging the distances that separated them.

In contrast to the customs of the stricter Old Order groups, the Texas Amish also embraced a more progressive approach. They held weekly services with Sunday school and actively supported missionary work.

As the buggy rattled along, Abner skillfully maneuvered the reins. The well-behaved mare responded with a gentle, rhythmic clip-clop. Abner's keen eye scanned for the perfect spot, one that would make it easy to hitch his horse and not obstruct the flow of others. With practiced ease, the old man brought the vehicle to a halt, the wheels coming to rest with a satisfying creak.

Abner pulled the brake, locking the buggy in place. "We made it," he declared, jumping down to tie up the horse. Once done, he helped his wife disembark. "Step lively now."

Joel and Olivia bounded out. Now that they were of age, they had the privilege of participating in the adult services, a milestone that filled them with pride and a sense of belonging.

"Wait, please," Isla called. She carefully adjusted her plain, black dress, smoothing the wrinkles that had formed during the bumpy ride. Long strands of hair had escaped her *kapp*, fluttering slightly around her face and neck with the breeze. Shading her eyes with a hand, she gazed around with a mixture of anticipation.

In the midst of the crowd, Evan's angular figure stood out. He stood beside Hazel, his tall frame casting a familiar silhouette. Though he wasn't dressed in traditional Amish garb, there was a quiet respectfulness to his appearance. His white shirt was buttoned to the collar, and a tailored vest hugged his frame. His slacks were crisply pressed, and his boots gleamed with a polished shine. His hair had been recently trimmed, the black strands neatly combed back to reveal the sharp lines of his face and the intensity in his dark gaze. He carried a wide-brimmed black hat, its presence a subtle nod to the world he had once known.

Isla's stomach fluttered, as if perhaps the day held more promise than she had anticipated. Despite everything he'd been through, Evan acted remarkably at ease.

"Look, *Mamm*! There's Sheriff Miller!" Olivia exclaimed.

"You think he'd want to play ball sometime soon?" Joel asked. "I really had fun." Gaze wistful, he clearly longed for a father figure to share in those small joys.

"You can always ask," Isla murmured, stealing another glance at Evan. His presence stirred something deep inside, reawakening an attraction she couldn't ignore. A thought emerged unbidden: he might someday be the kind of man who could fill the emptiness in their lives.

He'd make a wonderful father.

Warmth crept into her cheeks as she wrestled with her emotions. Evan's kindness and strength were undeniable, yet the traumas from his past loomed large, reminding her to tread carefully. Trust was hard-won, especially after everything she'd endured.

Evan turned suddenly, his gaze meeting hers. Nodding, he shared a few quick words with his aunt. Leaving Hazel to talk with friends, he wove his way toward her.

"*Guten morgen,*" he said in *Deitsch.*

Isla returned his greeting with a smile. "It's *gut* to see you here," she added. "How are you?"

"So far?" He shrugged, the movement loose and a little weary. "Just trying to get through." Hat in hand, he glanced at the ground before looking back up at her. "I, um… I wanted to thank you for being there. At the cemetery." His voice softened even more, as if the memory still pressed on him. "Talking to you helped sort a few things out."

"I'm glad to help. Anytime you need to talk, I'm always here."

"*Danke.*" His simple reply was laden with gratitude. Before the moment could deepen, the deacon's call to service echoed across the churchyard.

Evan straightened, clearing his throat as if to reset the moment. "Looks like it's time to head inside." He gave a quick wave to catch his aunt's attention.

Hazel hurried over. "Mind if we sit with you?"

"If you'd rather not, I understand," Evan added, glancing toward the gathering congregation.

"Of course you'll join us," Isla said. "I insist." Gathering Joel and Olivia, she guided them toward their destination.

As they neared the modest entrance, onlookers instinctively stepped aside, curiosity flickering in their eyes.

Though the crowd's whispers were too soft to fully discern, Isla felt a silent judgment in their stares. Something had changed, but she didn't know what.

Ready to greet all, Bishop Harrison's face broke into a smile, his gaze kind yet discerning. "*Gut* to see you, Sheriff Miller," he said, offering his hand. "It's been a while."

The lawman's expression softened, a flicker of gratitude crossing his face. "*Danke*, Bishop. Hope you don't mind me showing up."

The older man chuckled, the deep lines of his face creasing into a warm smile shaped by years of shepherding his flock through trials both great and small.

"Not at all, Sheriff. It's always a blessing to welcome those who protect our community. We can't truly know the weight of the job you carry, but we're grateful for your service."

Isla relaxed, her concern easing. Known for his sensible head and fair judgment, Clark Harrison never rushed to conclusions or let outside influences dictate his decisions. Instead, he led with a gentle hand, ensuring that even in their darkest moments, those in need could find a glimmer of hope.

She threw Evan a brief look. His gaze flickered with something that might have been relief.

He opened his mouth, but before he could respond, the peaceful moment was abruptly shattered.

A voice rang out, cutting through the air. "What blasphemy are you allowing into this holy place, Bishop?"

Chapter Nine

❧

Evan stood stiffly in Bishop Harrison's office. The faint smell of kerosene mixed with the musty odor of leather-bound volumes stirred memories that twisted his gut in knots. He hadn't been inside a church since he'd walked away, bitter and lost after Lila's death. Now, standing here, he wasn't sure if he'd come back to find healing or to confront the ghosts that had haunted him all these years.

His mind wound backward, replaying the brief scene that had stunned the entire congregation. Folks had gawked, eyes wide and faces pale with shock. Jonah Miller had always been a hard man, and the community knew better than to get between him and his son.

"You have no business here," Jonah had continued. "You left us long ago. Now stay gone!" But it wasn't just the accusation that cut deep. It was the look in his father's eyes. Hard. Unforgiving.

For a long moment, they'd stood locked in place, the space between them filled with everything unsaid, everything broken.

Evan hadn't expected to feel this much, hadn't expected the old hurt to rise like bile in his throat. Unwilling to fan the flames that were already burning too hot, he'd kept his mouth shut. Silence was safer. Arguing had never helped before, had only made things worse.

Thankfully, the bishop had had the wisdom to intervene. With a firm but gentle stance, Clark Harrison had stepped between the two men. He'd said nothing at first, but the strength of his presence alone had been enough to halt the heated exchange. Without saying anything, he'd gestured for the two men to follow him, moving them away from prying eyes and listening ears.

Delegating the service to a minister, the bishop led them into his office, shutting the door with a firm click. Whatever was said would remain private. The time for reckoning had arrived, and no one would leave until it was resolved.

Bishop Harrison took a seat behind his desk. "Now, we shall speak in calm tones." His lined face was stern as he looked between father and son. "You both agree, *ja*?"

Arms crossed, Jonah's eyes blazed. "There's nothing to speak of," he snapped, starting where he'd left off. "My *sohn* left our *familie*. Left his faith. And now he comes back as if he's one of us. As if he deserves to be here."

Evan swallowed hard. His quest for independence now loomed over him as a betrayal, leaving him to grapple with the reality that he might never fully belong again.

What if I can't be forgiven?

Bishop Harrison intervened. "That is a harsh accusation to throw at another man," he said, his gaze shifting between the two. "Your *sohn* deserves the right to defend himself."

Jonah harrumphed. "No *sohn* of mine would ever turn his back on *Gott*. We're *gut*, pious people, rooted in our respect to the Lord."

The bishop leaned forward slightly, his expression calm yet piercing. "I do not doubt that. But you seem to have forgotten that tolerance and forgiveness are the first things *Gott* expects of us all." He tilted his head, peering over the edge of his black frames, the light catching the silver strands in his hair. "You've not been a tolerant man, Jonah. And part of that is my fault. I've allowed this behavior to fester far too long."

"I have a right to my beliefs."

The bishop let out a soft sigh, a sound that seemed to carry years of countless prayers and heartaches.

"You're mistaken, Jonah. If you continue to deny your *sohn*, believing he has strayed, you do him a grave disservice. Unbaptized, Evan had every right to choose his own path. In those formative years, he needed your support, your blessing. Instead, you withdrew, replacing it with anger. Why? Because he dared to pursue a career in law enforcement?"

"He carries a gun," Jonah retorted, his voice trembling. "A weapon meant to take a life. How can I condone that when scripture warns us 'For all they that take the sword shall perish with the sword'?" His hand rose, pointing an accusatory finger. "And then...then..."

"Go on," Bishop Harrison urged. "We need to hear what you have to say."

Jonah's resolve suddenly crumbled. He sank into a nearby chair, his shoulders slumping as the fight drained from him. The anger that had fueled his actions evaporated, leaving behind a profound sense of loss and helplessness that enveloped him.

"What has this world come to?" he moaned. "Someone tried to kill my *sohn* for doing his job..."

And then it all made sense.

Evan felt the weight of his father's sorrow press down on him. Their estrangement wasn't just about his choices; it was about a love fraught with concern, an aching desire to protect what remained.

"*Daed*," he said, stepping closer. "I'm okay."

Jonah's gaze flickered. Stripped of all pretenses, his fear was laid bare for all to see. "You don't understand," he choked out. "Every time you went to work, I worried. I remember how the officers pulled up to the farm when Lila died. You think I wanted them to come again, to tell me you'd been killed?" Ashamed of the tears pooling in his eyes, he swiped them away with an angry hand. "And then they did come, telling me and your *mamm* that you'd been…"

The change struck Evan like a physical blow. Each word shaped the unspoken truth that hung between them. His father physically ached with the burden of the pain Evan had inflicted—not just on his *daed*, but on his *mamm*, too. And what of his younger brothers? He could only imagine the heavy toll the news had inflicted on their emotions.

"I didn't think you cared," he said softly.

Jonah's jaw clenched. "Well, you were wrong. I know that every time you went to work there was a chance you might never come back. Maybe you think I'm being unfair, but I'm speaking the truth, the kind that keeps me awake at night, praying you'll be safe." His gaze darkened, fear creeping into his eyes. "You don't understand what it does to a *vater*. Wondering when the day will come that his *sohn* is killed."

Bishop Harrison leaned forward, his presence calm but commanding in the charged atmosphere. "Jonah, we've heard the honesty in what you have to say. It takes a strong man to lay bare his soul as you have today. You've been through much, and yet here you stand, willing to confront what has been a burden for too long."

"Maybe I didn't show my feelings the way I should have," Jonah conceded. "But I'm doing it now, best I can."

The bishop's gaze never wavered as he turned to address Evan. "You've listened to your *vater*'s concerns. What will you do with that, knowing the truth of how he's felt?"

"*Daed*," he said, switching to *Deitsch*. "*Es tut mir so leid.* I didn't know you felt that way."

"You walked out when we needed you most," Jonah countered, shaking his head. "How was I supposed to feel? I'd just lost one child. Then I was losing another."

"I didn't think about that." At the time, he'd been too consumed by his own grief to see his parents' hearts were breaking, too. Instead, he'd charged forward, convinced he could fix everything. But all he'd discovered was that the world had no interest in being saved. And there was nothing he could do but accept the ashes.

The realization hit him hard. As the truth unspooled, Evan understood the cruel twist of fate: he was the villain in this narrative, the architect of his own downfall. Not only had he hurt the people he cared about, but he'd also lost sight of who he really was.

Silence fell hard, stretching out into an uncomfortable pause.

Bishop Harrison intervened. "Now that we're reached a reckoning, how do you propose proceeding?"

"I have no idea." Shoulders sagging, Evan glanced away. "There was a time I believed I'd chosen the right path. But lately, I've lost that certainty."

Bishop Harrison gave a gentle nudge. "Are you seeking to repair the bridges you've burned?"

Evan's throat tightened. "Desperately."

"But?"

"How does anyone know if God's really there?" he asked. "I mean, if He is, where is He?"

Jonah's face crumbled. "He's lost," his father pleaded. "He needs guidance. Please, help my *sohn* find his way back."

Bishop Harrison studied him, compassion etched into the lines of his face. "That's something a man has to find out for himself." He leaned forward, his weathered hands rested on the polished surface of the desk. "The journey back can be long and winding, but it's worth every step."

Evan felt anxiety squeeze. The air felt thicker, harder to breathe, as though it was pressing in on him from all sides. Healing would require more than words; it would demand a reckoning with the scars he'd inflicted—on himself and those around them.

"Where do I begin?" he asked, desperate for answers.

"You start with honesty," Bishop Harrison advised. "Speak your truth, even the ugly parts. Lay it bare before *Gott*, and you will find that grace is there waiting, ready to embrace you."

A flicker stirred inside him. The spark was

fragile, but it was there. For the first time in a long while, he felt as if he might just find his way back to the light.

Isla sat stiffly in the pew. The stillness of the church, normally a source of solace, now felt oppressive, thick with the unspoken tension that lingered in the air. The simple wooden benches, the faint creak of the floorboards beneath the congregation's weight and the lilting notes of the hymns did little to ease the unrest in her mind.

Her thoughts kept circling back to the confrontation between Evan and Jonah Miller earlier that morning. The feud between father and son had shattered the usual harmony of the peaceful gathering. She'd watched as Bishop Harrison, with his steady and calm presence, had quickly intervened, ushering the two men out of sight. The congregation, already familiar with the longstanding rift between them, had exchanged quiet glances but remained silent, trusting the bishop to resolve the matter.

When one of the ministers had stepped forward to announce that services would continue, the murmur of relief was palpable, though no one dared speak of the altercation aloud.

Yet Isla couldn't shake the scene from her mind. It wasn't just the quarrel. It was the deep-rooted pain behind it, the way Jonah's eyes had flickered with something akin to betrayal and

Evan's jaw had set in stubborn defiance. It wasn't the first time they'd clashed.

As the sermon commenced, Isla tried to concentrate on the minister's words. His voice, calm and steady, filled the room with reminders of conviction and forgiveness. Each verse and parable he spoke seemed to settle deep within her, a soothing balm for her weary soul.

Allowing herself to relax, she felt her worries begin to fade. Safe at church, surrounded by her community, she felt closest to *Gott*. His presence was as real as the sunbeams filtering through the open windows.

When the minister paused and the congregation rose to sing, Isla stood along with the others. Everyone opened their copies of the *Ausbund,* a songbook used for generations among the Amish. The books didn't contain musical notes; songs were learned and passed down from one generation to the next. A leader sang the opening notes of each line, after which the rest of the congregation joined in. Most of the hymns were slow with drawn-out notes. Each selection was an unbroken link to those who had gone before, their praise echoing through time.

Isla's voice blended with those around her, rising higher with every verse. The purity of the harmonies lifted her spirit, each note loosening the tension she had carried all week. The world's worries faded, and the beauty of the communal singing wrapped her in peace.

Just as she was becoming fully absorbed in the hymn, she noticed Jonah and Evan slipping quietly back into the service. Evan's shoulders were slightly hunched, his head lowered in deference as he moved to a bench near the rear of the room. Jonah followed, his posture stiff and formal, his face expressionless. Though they appeared calm, there was a subtle tension between them, an invisible thread of unease that hung in the air.

Though she had no way of knowing what had transpired behind closed doors, the fact that *vater* and *sohn* sat side by side was a small victory. For so long, Jonah had seemed distant, burdened by unhealed wounds. And Evan... Well, he had his own scars to bear.

Her fingers gripped the edges of her hymnal. She longed for answers, but the service wasn't over. Until it was, she could do nothing but wait.

Please, Lord, let them have come to peace.

As the last notes of the hymn faded into the stillness, a gentle hush fell over the congregation. Bishop Harrison appeared, stepping up to the podium. The morning sun poured through the tall windows, casting its warm glow over his weathered face.

With a warm, reassuring smile, Clark Harrison offered a brief apology for his absence. "Today, we gather not only to worship but also to strengthen the bonds that bind us as a community." He paused to gather his thoughts before continuing. "Let us continue this service in the spirit of unity."

As he spoke, the air seemed to shimmer with a sense of reverence, the congregation leaning in, eager to hear the message he'd prepared. To no one's surprise, his homily reminded people to lay down their disputes and come together in harmony.

Isla kept her eyes fixed forward, forcing herself to concentrate on the rest of the service, but it was an uphill battle. The soft murmurs of prayer and the gentle rustle of the congregation around her blurred into a background hum, overshadowed by her swirling thoughts.

An hour passed, and then another.

Finally, the three-hour service came to an end. The congregation rose from their benches, the room alive with movement and murmurs of conversation.

Normally, this was Isla's favorite part of the day. Enticing aromas wafted from the kitchen in the adjoining community rooms, where some of the women busily set up for the potluck luncheon.

Like other mothers, she rounded up her *youngies*. "Come, have something to eat," she urged, herding them toward the bustling gathering.

Joel, ever eager to play with his friends, raced ahead. Olivia lagged behind. Nearing thirteen, she was expected to help look after the younger children, a responsibility she took with the utmost seriousness.

As was custom, everyone threw themselves into the preparations. The men set up folding tables and chairs. Women tended the food and got the *kinder* settled.

Isla diligently collected and filled paper plates, ensuring everyone was served. Her own food lay untouched, forgotten. Lively chatter surrounded her, but she couldn't take a single bite. Pulse racing, she scanned the sea of faces.

Where is he?

Jonah Miller was easy to find, sitting alongside his *fraa*. Their three youngest boys clustered around them, each one a mirror of their father's sturdy frame and their mother's gentle spirit. Jonah appeared calm and steady as he spoke to his *familie*. Leah dabbed at her eyes with a handkerchief, the fabric crumpled in her grip. Hazel sat with them, too, wiping away the occasional tear.

Evan, however, was nowhere to be seen.

Isla searched the room again. Finally, she spotted him. Already halfway to the exit, his hat was pulled low over his brow.

Without thinking, she hurried after him, weaving through the clusters of people. "Hey," she called softly, careful not to draw too much attention to herself. "Wait for me."

He hesitated at the door, but didn't turn back.

"Evan," she called, quickening her pace.

At last, he stopped.

"Where are you going?" she asked.

"Outside to catch my breath. Need to clear my head."

"May I join you?"

Softening his guarded expression, Evan glanced at the crowd, then back at her. "I guess that would be all right."

As they stepped outside, a breeze ruffled the air. A nearby gazebo was nestled amidst a small grove of flowering trees. Adorned with climbing vines and colorful spring blooms, the gazebo served as a popular spot for couples to subtly declare their intentions under the watchful eyes of the community.

"Care to sit?"

"That would be nice," she agreed. Still, she felt a rush of self-consciousness as they approached. The gazebo, usually filled with laughter and whispers of budding romances, seemed suddenly daunting in its intimacy. She hesitated, glancing at the people milling around. Fortunately, most were too engrossed in their own conversations to pay any mind.

Taking a deep breath, she stepped inside and chose a seat on the weathered bench.

Her heart raced a little at the thought of sharing this private space with a man, even if just for a moment. She was acutely aware of her reputation, of the delicate balance between Amish and *Englischer*s.

Evan settled onto the bench across from her, maintaining a respectful distance. As he removed his hat, he absentmindedly toyed with the brim. "I guess you want to know what happened."

"The matter has crossed my mind."

"We've come to an understanding, my father and me. It's time to lay down our argument and let each other live in peace."

"Oh, that's wonderful."

He met her gaze, a hint of relief flickering in his eyes. "Yeah, it feels like it was meant to happen."

"I knew the Lord had plans. I've been praying you and Jonah would find peace and put your differences behind you."

"We both have our views on the matter, but I was able to see his side in a way I hadn't before."

"How so?"

"I never considered how my choice to work in law enforcement affected my family," he admitted. "It never crossed my mind that every time I went to work, I was putting them at risk too." He paused, staring into the distance. "But after what happened, being shot, feeling that fear of not knowing if I'd make it home, I finally understand. It's not just about me; it's about them, too. All these years, they've lived with the fear of getting that call… the one that says I didn't make it."

"I can't fault his reasoning. Though I do think the way he handled it was unreasonable."

"*Daed*'s never been good about sharing his feelings," he said. "He's always adhered to the stiff upper lip, just getting on with business. I never realized how deeply I had hurt him, taking off like I did after Lila's funeral. I didn't discuss it with anyone. I just made my decision and left."

Isla tilted her head, arching an eyebrow at him. "I'm aware."

She didn't need the reminder—she'd felt the sting of his choices more deeply than she'd ever admit aloud. Being left out of his plans had hurt. But it was the sense of not mattering that cut the deepest.

Evan's gaze dropped, shame creasing the lines of his face. "I handled everything badly," he admitted. "I hurt a lot of people. But especially you." His voice cracked a little. "You trusted me, and I shut you out like none of that meant anything. I was so wrapped up in what I wanted, I didn't stop to think about how much it would cost everyone else—how much it would cost you." He looked up at her then, his eyes searching hers. "I'm sorry. I know I can't take it back. All I can do is try to make things right."

Isla blinked, caught off guard by his honesty. Of all the things she'd hoped he'd say, she hadn't expected this, that he'd see her pain, and name it. The acknowledgment settled over her like a breath she hadn't known she'd been holding.

"It's never too late to start over," she said quietly.

"You think so?"

"I do," she said, her conviction growing stronger. "We all make choices that impact our families. It's how we respond and learn from those choices that truly matters."

Evan's shoulders relaxed, the tension that had coiled around him easing. "I have it on good authority the Lord believes in second chances. I just pray He's willing to give me one." His cautious optimism shone through, as though he were glimpsing the first rays of dawn after a long, dark night. Yearning sparked in the depths of his eyes, revealing the desire to embrace redemption with open arms.

Smiling, Isla blinked back tears. Watching someone take those first tentative steps toward a new life in devotion was always a powerful moment.

"I've no doubt," she murmured.

A comfortable silence enveloped them, punctuated only by the soft symphony of the afternoon.

In that moment, a sense of possibility filled the air. Tomorrow held the promise of renewal. Not just for Evan, but for her as well. With the weight of the past beginning to lift, she felt a spark of hope that tomorrow might bring healing and new beginnings.

Chapter Ten

Parked at the edge of the gravel driveway, Evan stared at the farm he'd left behind as a young man. He'd thought time would shrink the place in his memory, but it hadn't. If anything, it had grown larger in his absence, looming over him like the past he couldn't escape. The barn, painted a vibrant red, stood tall and proud against the flawless blue sky. Fenced-in pigpens lined the property, the sturdy wooden beams holding fast. The pigs, pink and brown, snuffled contentedly in the mud.

His gaze drifted to the house. The white clapboard siding gleamed in the afternoon sun, the porch swing swaying in the breeze. The smell of spring flowers in the garden mixed with the earthy scent of livestock, bringing a rush of memories he wasn't sure he wanted to face.

He slid out of the truck and headed that way. Each step felt heavier, bearing the years of absence. The mixture of damp earth and manure transported him back to the past, each memory heavier than the last. He clenched his fists, his nails digging into his palms as he approached his destination.

Before he could reach the door, it creaked open.

His mother appeared, her worn lavender dress fluttering. "*Mein sohn...*"

"*Mamm*," he managed, his throat tight.

In an instant, she was in his arms, hugging him like he was still her little boy. "You're home."

"I'm sorry I stayed away so long."

She pulled back, cupping his face. "You're here now. That's what matters."

Movement caught his eye. His father stood in the doorway, broad shoulders filling the frame. His face, lined with age and hard work, was unreadable, his beard reaching nearly to his chest.

"What took you so long?" His voice was calm, but the unspoken years lingered in the space between them.

Evan hesitated before responding, feeling the weight of those years pressing in. "I wasn't sure if you really meant what you said the other day." Standing here now, it was as if time had turned him back into that same frightened teenager, trying to make sense of a tragedy that had never truly let go.

His *daed* stepped forward, his eyes narrowing but not unkind. "Bishop Harrison told us to lay it down, and I did. I said my piece, and you know how I feel. When I said you could come back to the farm, I meant it." The old disappointment that had once hardened his gaze seemed to have softened, replaced by something else, something closer to understanding. But there was still a distance, a gap that couldn't be closed with just a few words.

Before he could respond, the sound of footsteps drew his attention. His three younger brothers emerged from the barn, their clothes streaked with mud, their faces flushed with surprise.

"Look who decided to show up!" James called, his sharp jawline reminding Evan just how much he resembled their father. He wiped his hands on his overalls as he approached, grinning despite the dirt.

"*Bruder*!" Matthias, the youngest, bounded up, clapping him on the back with an enthusiasm that hadn't changed since they were kids. "It's been too long!"

David, quieter than the others, smiled. "*Gut* to see you."

Evan managed a weak greeting. He'd expected this moment to feel like coming home, but it only reminded him how far he'd strayed.

Mamm, ever the peacemaker, stepped forward. "Let's go inside. I made fresh *kaffee* and there's cake."

"Sounds *gut*," he said, answering in *Deitsch*. It would be an insult to turn her down.

Inside the house, nothing had changed. The

same hand-stitched rugs covered the floors, the same wooden furniture filled the rooms. At the dining table, his brothers talked animatedly, filling the silence with stories of the farm.

Evan listened, but his heart wasn't in it. Every time the conversation drifted toward the future, toward their plans and hopes, his mind wandered back to Lila. She should have been here, too, her laughter mingling with theirs, her smile lighting up the room. Would she have been married by now? Would she have little ones of her own?

He clenched his jaw, pushing the thoughts away. The truth about what had happened that day loomed in his mind. Sooner or later, he'd have to speak up. It was the only way to heal, the only way to make things right.

Mamm busied herself at the kitchen counter, tending to the refreshments with efficient hands. "I hope you're hungry," she said, handing out the servings.

"I am. *Danke.*" Lifting his cup, he took a slow sip, savoring the familiar warmth. "I've missed this." No one could brew a pot like Leah Miller did. She had her own secret, adding a pinch of chicory to the grounds before letting the old percolator do its work. And her chocolate cake with double fudge icing was a slice of pure comfort. The first bite melted on his tongue, a perfect match for the *kaffee*'s slightly bitter edge.

Conversation continued in a pleasant yet hollow rhythm, the warm smiles and friendly chatter masking an undercurrent of buzzing tension. Eventually someone had to broach the subject they'd all hoped to avoid.

But Evan was ready. Or at least, he thought he was.

Giving him a curious look, Matthias broke the fragile peace. "How's your arm?"

"Healing fine. Barely know it happened."

"You sure had us worried," David said.

"Ain't a *gut* feeling seeing a deputy pulling up in the driveway," James chimed in, shaking his head.

Daed gave a sharp glance. "We don't need to talk about it."

"You'll be going back to work soon, *ja*?" *Mamm* asked.

Appetite fading, Evan lowered his fork. His job had once been a calling, something that defined him. But now, as he spent more time away, he started to wonder if it was still the life he wanted. What if there was something else, something he'd been too busy to see, too consumed by duty to consider?

The idea of returning felt less like a certainty and more like a question.

What had he been chasing all these years? And was it worth the price?

"I'm not sure," he said simply.

Silence fell over the gathering. Even his brothers stopped talking, the significance of his words sinking in.

Daed's brow furrowed. "What does that mean?"

"It means I'm thinking about finding something else to do after my term is up."

Mamm's reaction was instant. Her hand flew to her heart, eyes brightening with hope. "Are you really going to, *sohn*?"

Daed leaned forward, propping himself on his elbows. "That's a big decision. But I can't say I wouldn't be glad if you did."

Evan hesitated. The idea of disappointing them was like a boulder sitting on his chest.

"I've had a lot of time to think since I've been off. About the things I left behind and about who I was before Lila passed."

The air thickened, the clatter of forks halting midair as his sister's name hung in the silence, swallowing the warmth of the moment.

Daed's expression darkened. *Mamm's* breath hitched.

"I have to tell you all something," he continued. "Something I should have a long time ago."

"What is it?" David asked.

"The day Lila died, I was the one to blame for the accident." The memory of the withered bouquet at her grave clung to him, a lingering presence he couldn't shake. Had it been left as a strange expression of sympathy—or as a silent accusation of his culpability? He still didn't know who had placed it there. Or why.

Mamm gave a puzzled look. "What do you mean?"

"Don't know why we have to talk about this," *Daed* interrupted.

"I do have to talk about it," Evan said, pressing on. "I wasn't the one driving the wagon. Lila was. We switched places. I let her take the reins." He swallowed hard, the bitter taste of bile choking him. "Then the truck came, and everything happened so fast." His voice dropped to a whisper. "I was supposed to be sitting where she was. It should've been me."

There it was. For years, he'd buried the events of the day beneath layers of self-loathing. His hands shook, the phantom weight of a bottle long gone still pressing against his palm, a reminder of the nights spent drowning in regret. And yet, the whiskey hadn't freed him. It had only imprisoned him further.

He waited for the explosion, for the anger, the accusations.

But none came.

Dismay etched his father's brow. "Why didn't you tell us?"

"I was scared," he blurted, his voice cracking under the strain. "I couldn't face it. Couldn't face you." Half babbling, he pushed his chair back, the scrape of wood against the floor echoing his turmoil. "I'm sorry. I know I did everything wrong. I should go."

Daed reached out, placing a hand on his shoulder. The touch was grounding, a reminder that despite the chaos, there was still a bond between them. "Just sit a minute. I'm not mad. Just thinking."

A twisting pressure knotted his insides, sharp and relentless. "I don't deserve to be welcomed. Not after what I did."

"We all make mistakes," *Daed* replied. "But running from them won't fix anything. If anyone deserves harsh judgment, it's me. I claim to live by *Gottes wort*, but I couldn't find it in my heart to understand the trauma you'd been through. If I had just tried to listen, we might have had a more peaceable settlement about your choices."

"It wasn't your fault," *Mamm* reassured him. "Lila knew how to handle a wagon as *gut* as you did. Maybe even better."

Tears stung Evan's eyes. He blinked them back, the lump in his throat too big to swallow. "If we hadn't changed places, Lila might still be alive."

"Accidents are part of life," *Daed* countered. "Sometimes, no matter what we do, the worst still happens. We're not always in control. And we're not meant to be."

"You're not the only one who's struggled," David admitted. "We've all been carrying the weight of Lila's loss."

James spoke up. "She wasn't even supposed to go with you. I was. But I was lazy and didn't want to ride in that hot, open cart."

"If I hadn't been so slow to get the horse hitched up, you'd have been on time," Matthias added, shamefaced.

Raising a hand, *Mamm* glanced between her four sons. "You can sit here blaming yourselves all day. But the truth is, it was all in *Gott's* hands. It always has been, and it always will be."

Evan felt something inside him break, and relief came crashing in. He'd expected anger. He'd braced himself for judgment. But instead, his family was offering something he hadn't dared hope for.

Understanding.

"I made a lot of mistakes, and hurt a lot of people," he admitted. "If I could go back, I'd do everything differently."

"Such as?" *Daed* asked.

"I'd have stayed Amish." Leaving had cost him everything that mattered. If it weren't for the fact that the man who shot him was still out there, he'd go ahead and hand in his resignation without a second thought. But as it stood, he felt caught between his duty as sheriff and his longing to live in a way that truly honored the Lord.

Mamm gave him long look. "You *are* Amish, *sohn*," she said softly. "You always have been. You just haven't committed yourself. And the door to that choice is always open."

"I want to," he said. "But I'm having trouble with believing there is a higher power. Lila didn't deserve to die. And I can't wrap my head around a God who would allow something like that to happen. If there's supposed to be some divine plan, then why do the good people get hurt?"

"Being firm in our belief is never easy." *Mamm*'s hand brushed against his arm, a warm and reassuring gesture. "We all struggle with it. And you can't blame *Gott* either. He gives us burdens, *ja*, but He also gives us the strength to carry them. If we let Him."

"What if I can't do it? What if the Lord won't have me back?"

His mother's gaze didn't falter. "You won't be alone. None of us walk this path by ourselves. Lean on *Gott*. He doesn't ask for perfection. All He asks for is your heart."

"I want to—" His voice broke before he could finish.

Mamm rose, moving to wrap her arms around him. "Then that's all you need to do. Try. *Gott* will do the rest."

The rhythmic whirring of the sewing machine filled Isla's workshop as she guided the fabric through the presser foot, her hands moving with precision. The room smelled faintly of linen and beeswax, the latter used to keep her threads from tangling. Sunlight streamed through the window, casting its glow on the neat rows of fabric bolts lined up along the wall, every color of the rainbow folded and stacked like promises yet to be fulfilled. She leaned back, rubbing her tired neck, and caught sight of the clock.

It was nearly noon.

Not that time mattered much to her these days. The routine of working, taking care of her children and maintaining her home kept her grounded. Commissions had been distressingly thin lately, leading her to consider finding employment outside the home. But she wasn't accustomed to working in the public sphere and stepping into it felt daunting. Outside of sewing, she had little practical experience that would bring in money. What would she even do?

The enormity of her worries pressed on her. The room seemed too quiet, the ticking of the clock on the wall too loud, too sharp against the backdrop of her swirling thoughts.

Her gaze drifted to the worn Bible on the side table, its cover soft from years of use. She rose, crossing the room to retrieve it. She sank back into her chair, opening the pages to a familiar passage. *Be still and know that I am God.*

The passage filled her with a quiet calm, but uncertainty still lingered. She closed her eyes, folding her hands over the Bible in her lap, and whispered a prayer.

"Dear Father, I feel so lost right now. You've

blessed me with these gifts, with my *youngies*, with this life, but I'm struggling and it's hard to see the way forward. Please, Lord, show me what I should do. I know You provide in all things, and I trust You to guide my path. Give me the courage to step where You lead, even if it's into the unknown. Help me find peace in Your plan."

She didn't have all the answers yet, but the prayer had brought her comfort. Even in these uncertain times, His plan would unfold, even if she couldn't see it yet.

The rumble of tires on gravel before the faint knock at the door pulled her out of her thoughts. Isla set the Bible aside and rose.

Evan waited outside. Dressed in faded jeans and a plain white shirt, his Stetson was pulled low, shading his eyes. The cautious smile on his lips hinted at something unspoken.

"Am I interrupting?"

"No," she said. "Nothing I can't set aside."

"I was just wondering…" Fidgeting uncomfortably, he stuffed his hands into his pockets. "I know you've got things to do, but would you care to grab some lunch?"

His invitation sent a flutter through her chest. A part of her longed for the escape, to leave the confines of the *haus* even if just for a little while. It would be a refreshing break from her usual routine. But lunch with him? That was something entirely different. It wasn't customary for an Amish woman to spend time with an *Englisch* man unless her husband or brother was present. The thought of it felt reckless, a departure from the careful lines she lived by.

She hesitated, feeling the pressure of tradition. "I wasn't planning on going out."

"I understand," he said. "But I guarantee, my intentions are honorable. There's something I need to talk to you about. I wouldn't ask otherwise."

That gave her pause. His eyes held a sincerity she couldn't ignore. "All right. But I can't be gone long. The *kinder* are in school, and I want to be here when they come home

"I wouldn't ask you to stay longer than you're comfortable."

"Actually, I could use a break. Give me a few minutes to get ready." Having lunch with a friend in public couldn't stir up too much gossip, could it? And if it did, well, people had small lives if they found this worth talking about.

He smiled. "Great."

Isla turned and slipped back inside. Reaching for her shawl, she wrapped it around her shoulders. Glancing in the mirror, she adjusted her *kapp*, fingers brushing over the fabric as she made sure it was straight. Satisfied, she reached for her purse, a colorful patchwork bag crafted from pieces of scrap material.

Stepping outside, she found Evan waiting by his

truck. The engine hummed, a sound that seemed oddly foreign compared to the quiet simplicity of her usual life. When he opened the door, she hesitated only a moment before climbing into the passenger seat.

"I'm not used to riding in these things." The smooth leather felt strange beneath her, and the seat belt, though necessary, made her feel slightly trapped.

Evan grinned as he climbed in. "Don't worry, I'll take it easy."

Isla smiled, feeling a little of the tension melt away. As they rolled away from the curb, she watched the familiar sights pass by.

The drive was short, but the destination was a familiar one. Amish-owned, the drive-in had an uncommon twist: parking for buggies, complete with hitching posts for the horses. It was a nice touch that gave Amish teens on *Rumspringa* a place to hang out with friends without taking them too far away from traditional values.

A flicker of memory stirred. "This place…"

He grinned. "Been a long time since we've hung out here together," he said, pulling into a space reserved for gas-powered vehicles.

A touch of nostalgia filled her. "I've never forgotten." They had been just kids then, hopeful, innocent and dreaming of a future that never came to pass.

"I thought it'd be nice to revisit," he said.

A carhop hurried over. "What'll ya have?" she asked, pen poised above her order pad.

Evan glanced over. "Remember what we ordered?"

She laughed. "Cheeseburgers with Tater Tots, and chocolate milkshakes. Hold the onions."

"Make it two," he said, ordering the same meal they'd shared all those years ago.

The carhop snapped her gum. "Be about ten minutes."

Evan leaned back, his eyes trailing after the carhop until she disappeared. "I went by the farm yesterday."

"You did?"

"Yeah."

"How did it go?" she asked.

"Better than I expected. We talked for the first time in years. *Daed* forgave me." His eyes flicked up to meet hers, a shadow of vulnerability in them. "I'm trying. I'm really trying to find my way back."

"Back to the community?"

"*Ja*. It's not easy. I've been gone so long, lived in ways that I'm not proud of." He hesitated, his hand rubbing at the back of his neck. "I'm kind of in a twelve-step program now."

She blinked. "A twelve-what?"

Evan offered a faint, almost self-conscious smile. "A twelve-step program. It's something they use in the *Englisch* world for people who are recovering."

"Recovering from what?"

His gaze drifted away. "An addiction to alcohol."

Isla's stomach sank. Since the day of the fundraiser, she'd wondered if the subject would come up. Of course, she hadn't wanted to believe Andrea Richards was speaking the truth.

"You're an alcoholic?"

"I am," he confessed, his voice firm but not defensive. "But I'm sober now. Almost four months."

"What made you stop?"

A flicker of regret shadowed his face. "The night Hazel fell, I was on one of my rare days off. I didn't check on her that weekend because I was, um, indisposed. She lay there alone until a neighbor found her the next day. That was the moment I realized I could have lost her. I couldn't let that happen again. So, I quit."

"I think that's an admirable thing," she said. "Admitting you have a problem and addressing it."

"You don't act surprised."

"I'm not."

He winced. "I guess people talk."

"Things get around in a small town," Isla said, offering no further details. No reason to make it harder than it already was. "But knowing about it doesn't mean that I judge you. It means I understand everyone has their battles." His desire to recover moved her, far more than he knew.

Evan let out a hollow laugh. "Well, that went easier than I thought it would."

"Is there a reason you're telling me?"

"There is. Part of the program is making amends with the people you've hurt," he explained. "That includes you."

"Does it?"

"I made mistakes," he said. "I wasn't fair to you, not back then. I left without explaining. I didn't even give you a chance to understand why." He hesitated, running a hand over his face. "I want you to know I intend to fix that."

"Oh? How?"

His fingers curled around the steering wheel. "With all that's happened, it's got me to thinking about what I want for the future. I haven't been happy, and I think it's because I don't belong in the *Englisch* world." He took a deep breath to steady himself. "I've decided to start rebuilding my life, as an Amish man."

Isla's hands shook as she folded them in her lap. The raw honesty in his voice, was different from the brash, impulsive boy she had once known.

"Are you sure?"

"I am."

Her thoughts spun, trying to make sense of the flood of emotions, the implications of what this could mean. "Evan, this is so…unexpected."

"A *gut* thing, I hope."

She smiled. "*Ja*, it is."

Evan hesitated, then met her gaze with a vulnerability she hadn't seen in years. "There's something else I'd like you to consider."

Anticipation flickered. "And that is?"

"What would you think about starting over?" he asked. "You know, giving me another chance?"

Caught in a whirlwind of emotions, Isla's pulse quickened. His question lingered in the space between them, weighted with memory and possibility.

Could they make things work, after all these years?

Chapter Eleven

Evan stood at the gate of Bishop Harrison's house. The journey he'd been on had led him here, though the path had been long and uncertain. But he'd come to a decision, one that felt right deep in his bones. With a firm movement, he released the latch and walked forward, his resolve solidifying with each step.

The door creaked open before he had a chance to knock. The bishop's weathered face broke into a warm smile. Dressed in simple black pants, suspenders and a plain white shirt, Clark Harrison embodied everything he admired in the Amish: the simplicity, the conviction, the peace.

"It's *gut* to see you again," he said, his voice strong despite his age. "Come inside."

"*Danke*." Evan stepped into the house, the familiar scent of woodsmoke greeting him. It was a small house, modest and uncluttered.

"Please, sit." The bishop directed him to the living room, indicating he should take a seat.

Miriam Harrison peeked out of the kitchen.

"I see we have company," she said in greeting. "Would you like something to drink?"

"I've just come to talk to Clark," Evan said, shaking his head. "I wouldn't want to be a bother."

"Nonsense. I'll have something out in a minute."

Disappearing into the kitchen, she soon emerged balancing a tray brimming with treats. Two tall glasses of iced tea were accompanied by a saucer filled with anise nut cookies.

"I hope you enjoy these," she said. "I made them this morning." An Amish treat that resembled biscotti, the cookies had a satisfying crunch on the outside, giving way to a tender, chewy center that promised a burst of flavor with every bite.

Evan accepted her offering. "*Danke.*"

Miriam stepped back. "I'll be out in the garden if you need anything else," she said, before quietly slipping out.

A hush settled between the two men.

Evan politely sipped his tea, then set the glass down. "Thank you for agreeing to see me today."

Clark Harrison raised an eyebrow, a hint of a smile playing at the corners of his lips. "I could hardly refuse. You sounded like you needed to talk."

"I do," he admitted. "Some of the things you mentioned during our meeting on Sunday have been weighing heavily on my mind. I wanted to explore those thoughts further."

"Sounds reasonable," the bishop said, leaning back in his chair. "I'm here to help in any way I can."

"I'm thinking about returning to the church," he blurted.

"I had a feeling that was on your mind."

"It's something I've thought about for a long time, but it's only recently that I realized I'm ready to make the change." Returning to the Amish wasn't just about changing the way he lived. It was about healing the brokenness inside him, finding peace after years of turmoil.

"It's a big decision." Concern etched the older man's face, his brow furrowing. "One that will require time, patience and a deep commitment."

"I know it won't be easy. But I'm ready to do whatever it takes."

"Why now? After so many years?"

Evan froze. He'd rehearsed the answer a hundred times. But now the words he'd planned to say seemed inadequate. Still, he tried.

"I thought I knew what I wanted. But these last few years, it feels like I've lost my way. Things I thought would make me happy didn't. I've spent years chasing something I can't even name, but all it's done is leave me feeling empty."

"The *Englisch* world makes many promises," the bishop said quietly. "But it rarely delivers what the soul truly needs."

No disagreement there. "I miss the peace. I

miss the simplicity. And I miss having *Gott* in my life," he said. "I don't know how else to explain it."

"You don't need to. I've seen this before, many times. The pull of the secular world can be strong, but so is the strength of our Lord."

"I want to come back," Evan continued. "I know it won't be easy, and I know there's a lot I need to change, but I'm ready."

Bishop Harrison lifted a hand, not to bless, but to halt. "Returning isn't as simple as you might think."

Evan froze. That raised hand felt like a wall, immovable and final.

"I understand," he replied. "I'm ready to put in the work."

"Are your parents aware of your desire?"

"*Ja.* I went back to the farm the other day. *Daed* and I had a long talk. I finally understand why he was so angry. It wasn't just about me walking away. It was like I turned my back on everything he believed in."

"Jonah grew up in Ely's Bluff. Folks there cling tightly to the belief that there's no living outside of their *Ordnung*," Bishop Harrison said. "I've spoken to him many times about you, but he wouldn't hear it. I prayed *Gott* would open his heart. I'm so grateful that He finally has."

"Me, too. I've missed having family around… being part of the community." Things weren't perfect between himself and his father. But it was getting better. With time, he hoped to mend the rift completely, to heal the wounds that had lingered for too long.

"Are you sure this is what you want?" The bishop's voice was calm but edged with gravity. "If I agree to counsel you, I'd expect you to follow through. That will mean changing everything about your life and sticking to it. That will include changing your job."

Evan nodded. Keeping his current profession was never going to be an option. And, when the time came, he was prepared to make that sacrifice.

"Absolutely. Just tell me what to do."

"You're going to have to shed *Englisch* ways," the bishop continued. "It's a process. One step at a time. I don't expect you to change everything at once. But you'll need to relearn what it means to live by our ways."

"I'm ready for that. I've discussed the matter with Levi Wyse a time or two," he said. "He told me what it was like for him, coming back after all those years. Caleb Sutter, too. He didn't even know he was born Amish until after he was grown, but he was able to make the changes."

"I'm not saying it's impossible." The bishop's gaze sharpened, assessing him. "But it won't be easy. Being a lawman, you're carrying a lot of extra baggage others have not. Letting go of the oath you took to serve and protect may prove harder than you think."

Evan rubbed a hand over his jaw. "I've been thinking about that," he admitted. "I've been looking into finding an accredited EMT program."

The bishop's brow lifted. "EMT?"

"Emergency medical technician," he said. "I know it's not a typical job for an Amish man, but I believe it's something I'm meant to do. I do have some basic medical training. I'd like to expand on that and use that skill to serve others."

"It's not the usual path," Bishop Harrison countered. "However, the Amish have always valued helping in times of need."

"I could still be of service to the public, but without the weight of a gun on my hip. No more violence. I just want to help save lives."

"You have an admirable ambition. And, given your unique circumstances, I would certainly allow it. More Amish are going on to further their educations nowadays and branching into non-traditional careers while still maintaining their ties to the church."

"I was hoping you would say that."

"As the world changes, we must find ways to adapt without sacrificing our beliefs," the bishop continued. "But I'm afraid it won't make your path any easier. The skills and tools you've relied on for so long—well, letting go of your authority won't come naturally."

"I know. But if I don't try, I'll always wonder what kind of man I could've been. Who I might become if I can make it work."

There. He'd said it all, laid bare the need that had driven him to this moment.

Silence hung in the air, thick and unyielding, each second dragging on, testing the fragile thread of hope he'd dared to spin.

Worry swamped him. *What if he says no?* What if there was no path to redemption? The burden of his failures pressed hard. The bishop could very well refuse and turn him away.

At last, the church elder broke the silence, his voice soft but still laden with authority. "If you feel this is where *Gott* is calling you, then I support it."

Relief filled him. "*Danke.*"

"I believe your heart is in the right place," the bishop continued. "However, my biggest concern right now is your faith. Walking closely with Christ is the cornerstone of who we are and what we live for."

Evan swallowed hard, feeling exposed, as if the older man could see straight into the deepest recesses of his soul. "I understand that."

Clark Harrison leaned forward, his weathered hand resting gently on the well-worn leather Bible between them. His voice was steady, filled with quiet conviction. "In Romans, it says if you declare with your mouth and believe in your heart that Jesus Christ is Lord, you will be saved. But it's not just the words. It's about surrender. True surrender. It starts with accepting Christ into your life, opening yourself to His will. Are you willing to do that?"

"I am. I want that."

The bishop smiled softly, the lines around his eyes deepening. "*Gut.* That's the first step. But it's between you and the Lord now. I can't do this for you. Find a quiet spot, somewhere you feel close to *Gott.* Kneel, open your heart and tell Him everything. Ask for forgiveness. And then listen. Really listen to what the Lord has to say to you."

Emotion swelled within him. "I understand." He'd spent years pushing away the notion of a higher power, building walls of skepticism and anger. The thought of stopping long enough to listen felt like the hardest thing he'd ever be asked to do. Yet deep down, something stirred. A faint whisper, almost imperceptible, told him that this was exactly what he needed.

"Do you have a Bible?" the bishop asked.

"I do. *Mamm* gave me one when I was younger. I still have it."

"*Gut.* Keep it close. Let it guide you, especially in the hard times. The answers you seek, the peace you need—it's all in there."

"I'm ready." And he was. It was time to embrace the Lord's word and finally live by it.

"You'll need a sponsor. Someone to guide you through this journey, step by step. I'm willing to take on that role, if you're open to it."

Evan blinked, startled by the offer. A surge of gratitude rushed through him, unexpected and overwhelming. "I'd be honored."

Bishop Harrison gave an approving nod. "We'll take it slow. You'll change one thing at a time, and when you're comfortable, you'll move on to the next. There's no rush. This is about transformation, not speed. Most candidates who've lived *Englisch* usually need a year to make the adjustments. Sometimes longer."

Evan slowly exhaled. "I'll do whatever you recommend."

Finding a shady spot beneath a grove of towering trees, Isla carefully spread a checkered blanket across the thick wild grass. Light filtered through the leaves above, creating a patchwork of shadows that played on the fabric. A gentle breeze carried the distant laughter of children and the faint melody of birdsong.

With the blanket in place, she looked over at the horse and buggy parked nearby. When Evan had invited her and the *kinder* for a day out, she'd expected him to roll up in his truck. Instead, he'd arrived in a more traditional vehicle, the gentle clip-clop of the horse's hooves and the rhythmic creaking of the wooden wheels announcing his arrival.

He leaned into the vehicle, his shoulders momentarily hidden as he rummaged inside. Emerging with a wicker picnic basket that looked almost too large for one man to carry, he strode toward her, a smile lighting up his face.

"I hope everyone's hungry," he said, his tone playful as he set the basket down. "I think Hazel packed everything but the kitchen sink."

Isla chuckled. "Knowing Hazel, that wouldn't surprise me."

"She insisted. I had no say." He jerked a thumb toward the buggy. "And I know you have to be wondering about that contraption."

"I didn't think I'd ever see you in one again."

"The bishop told me I needed to change one thing at a time. That's my thing. I've got to start learning how to get around without my truck. I haven't ridden in anything a horse would pull since…well, since Lila died."

"How do you feel about that?" she asked.

"To be honest, I think they're not that safe, even with all the new features to make them more visible. But I realized I can't let my anxieties keep me captive." He glanced at the buggy, its black wooden frame weathered from sitting out in the elements. "Hazel hasn't used it much since *Onkel* Gideon passed. Getting that thing hitched up and rolling again was quite a challenge. Old Bessie sure wasn't happy to be back in a harness."

"I can't imagine what you'll change next."

Evan raised a brow, a faint smile tugging at the corners of his mouth. "Probably my clothes. I'll have to give up the jeans and T-shirts." He glanced down at himself. "It'll feel strange putting on those things again."

"I think you'll look just fine." The image of him donning those simple garments ignited a warmth in her chest. It wasn't just about the clothing; it was about his commitment to follow through with his promises.

"Guess I'll need to go shopping soon, since I don't have a *fraa* to make my clothes." He gave a sly wink, a playful glint in his eyes. "At least, not yet."

Isla felt a flush creep up her cheeks. For a fleeting moment, she let her imagination wander, picturing what it would be like to be his wife. A smile tugged her lips as she envisioned him beside her, his laughter filling their kitchen, their hands intertwined as they navigated the challenges of their lives. Would he always look at her like that, with such warmth and promise?

Lost in her daydream, the joyful sounds of children at play brought her back to reality.

Joel, his cheeks flushed with excitement, held tightly to the string of a bright blue kite. It soared high above him, dancing playfully in the sky.

Nearby, Olivia was a picture of pure joy, her laughter echoing as she ran with her fiery red kite. With every gust, it dipped and climbed.

The wide-open space allowed the children to run freely, their feet pounding against the soft earth as they chased the wind. Both were completely absorbed in the game, their excitement infectious as they celebrated the simple pleasure of flight beneath the bright sky.

"Look, *Mamm*! Mine's the highest!" Olivia yelled, her voice bubbling with delight as she tugged on the string.

Joel, not to be outdone, pulled at his own string, determined to make his kite dance even higher. "Mine's going to touch the clouds!"

Waving back, Isla's heart swelled with warmth at the sight. Months ago, grief had weighed heavily on them. Losing their father had cast a long shadow over their lives. The recent aftermath of the robbery also lingered, a reminder of how quickly peace could be shattered. Yet in that moment, the fear seemed distant. For now, they seemed to be reclaiming the joy that had been so elusive lately.

"Looks like they're having fun."

"They are. *Danke* for planning a day out for them. It means more than you know."

"I thought they could use a break."

"After everything, I just want them to feel normal again," she said. "To be happy."

Evan gave her a long look. "I want you to be happy, too."

A blend of excitement and apprehension spread through her. When she'd agreed to see him again, she'd made no firm commitment. They'd agreed to keep things casual, building on a foundation of friendship. Now that he was attending church and had begun counseling with the bishop, it wasn't technically forbidden for them to spend time together. He'd made his intentions to return to the Amish clear. So far, he was following through with each step, proving his commitment. Not just to the community, but to her as well.

Still, a cautious voice echoed in her mind, urging her to take each moment as it came. He had many hurdles ahead. Staying sober, adjusting to Amish customs and rebuilding his life from scratch were just a few of the challenges looming over him.

"Evan, I—"

He held up a hand. "I know. No promises." A smile crept across his face, brightening his eyes. "'Take therefore no thought for the morrow: for the morrow shall take thought for the things of itself.'"

Recognizing the quote from Matthew, Isla smiled. "Been studying up, have you?"

"The bishop gave me some lessons to start on."

She studied him, curiosity piqued. "How do you feel about that?"

"Like I'm getting to know the Lord all over again. It's comforting, reminding me that I'm not alone in this." His gaze softened as he spoke, continuing, "Even when I stumble, there's always a way back."

"That's true. The Lord's grace knows no end."

"I felt ashamed for turning away for so long, blaming *Gott* for everything," he admitted. "But it was all on me. Knowing I'm forgiven brings me peace."

Isla's thoughts drifted back to her own struggles. "It's easy to feel lost sometimes. I've been there myself. After the break-in, I couldn't understand why *Gott* would let the thief take all I had. But I see now the money was nothing important. Our needs have been met in ways I couldn't have imagined, and we've never gone without."

"It's reassuring, isn't it? Knowing we're not alone, even in our darkest moments."

"Amen," she replied.

Shaking off his melancholy, he glanced toward Joel and Olivia. "What do you say we join them?"

She laughed. "Why, I haven't flown a kite since I was a girl."

"It's not just for the *youngies*." He held out his hand in an inviting way. "Come on."

Isla hesitated, glancing at her children. The thought of joining them in something carefree sparked a flicker within her.

"Why not?"

"Great. I hoped you'd say that, so I bought an extra one." Jogging to the buggy, he went to retrieve it.

They walked together toward the open field.

Away from the trees, Evan unwrapped a vibrant kite adorned with swirling patterns. With a few deft movements, he pieced it together before attaching a long roll of string.

"Let's see if we can make it soar." He took a step back, his gaze fixed on the open sky. "Hold it steady," he instructed, unraveling more string.

Isla clutched the kite's frame, feeling the gentle pull from the wind. "Okay."

As the breeze picked up, he called out, "One… two…three… Let it go!" With a swift motion, he let the string slip through his fingers and then tugged hard.

Isla released the kite. It caught the breeze and leaped high, its colors bursting against the canvas of the sky.

"Look at it go!" Nearby, Joel and Olivia's kites added more splashes of color.

Evan released more string, allowing the kite to glide effortlessly above. "All yours," he said, handing over the spool.

Isla's pulse accelerated as his hand brushed hers. The wind whispered around them, and for a moment, it felt like the world had shrunk down to just the two of them. Somehow it all felt right.

Tipping her head back, she closed her eyes

and let the warmth of the sun envelop her. For one giddy moment, she felt young and alive, unburdened by her responsibilities, free from the shadows. The children's laughter faded into the background as she allowed herself to dream of a future brimming with promise.

He nudged her shoulder with his. "Penny for your thoughts."

Isla reluctantly opened her eyes. "I was thinking about where life might take us next."

A thoughtful expression etched itself across his face. "I've been making plans. You know, for what I'll do after I leave office."

"Oh?" It made sense, she realized. Returning to the Amish would almost certainly mean he'd have to abandon law enforcement. "What are you going to do?"

"I thought about going back to the farm, working with *Daed* again. But you know me and pigs. Hambone is about all the swine I can handle."

"He is cute, though."

"The exception, not the rule." He laughed. "Anyway, I'm looking into other career options. I've talked to the bishop and he agrees with my choice. I'll still be helping people, but in a different way."

"You're sure that's what you want?"

"Yeah. I do," he replied, his voice steady. "I'll be able provide for myself. And Lord willing—"

he met her gaze, the intensity of his look sending a shiver down her spine "—a family."

Isla felt the oxygen drizzle from her lungs.

Is he talking about our future…together?

The kite suddenly jerked, sending a rush of exhilaration through her.

She'd loved Evan once. Deeply. And if she were honest, she'd never truly stopped. Did he have any idea how fiercely she still cared? How desperately she longed for the very same things: love, stability and the warmth of a home filled with harmony?

Her pulse thudded faster, a frantic rhythm in her ears. The truth slammed into her.

She wasn't just falling for Evan again.

She'd already fallen.

Completely and irrevocably.

Chapter Twelve

Interim Sheriff Diego Lopez leaned back in his chair, his fingers steepled in front of him. A three-year veteran of the department, he was capable, sharp and already making a name for himself. Yet beneath his composed exterior, a subtle tension flickered in his eyes, betraying the strain of the responsibility he now carried.

"I imagine you know why I asked you to come in today," Lopez began.

Evan met the man's gaze. "I've got an idea."

Attempting to maintain his calm, Lopez flipped open the folder on his desk. "I'll cut to the chase and let you know the investigation into your use of force and firearm discharge is complete."

"And?" he asked, bracing himself.

"You've been exonerated."

A slow trickle of relief washed over Evan, but it barely eased the tight coil of tension in his gut. The suspect had been armed and desperate, willing to do anything to escape. Still, despite the official validation that he'd acted in self-defense, a lingering unease gnawed at him.

"I'm glad to hear you say that." In the chaos of the confrontation, he'd relied on instinct. Drawing his weapon had never been something he did lightly. It was always the last resort, the one decision no lawman ever wanted to make.

Lopez shuffled more paperwork. "I've also reviewed the reports from your doctors with the county commissioners. You've kept up with your appointments, and that's commendable. It's not easy having someone dig through every part of your life, but it's necessary."

"I'm aware." The county had protocols to ensure he was healthy, not just physically but mentally. "What's the word?"

"Dr. Keller and Dr. Rhyland have both cleared you. Based on their recommendations, you're fit for duty."

Relieved, Evan allowed himself to relax. *It's over.*

When the incident first happened, the plan had been simple. He'd recover and then return to the job like nothing had changed.

But everything had changed.

As the weeks slipped by, his perspective had shifted, subtly at first, then all at once. Immersing himself in the rhythms of Amish life had stirred something deep within him. He found himself picturing a different kind of future. Quiet Sunday mornings at church, walking hand in hand with Isla, children chattering at their sides. Laughter around the dinner table. Peace at night.

Shaking his head, he let the thoughts go. Such things were only a dream for now, just out of reach. He had responsibilities he couldn't set aside. Not yet, anyway.

"I'll do my best not to let anyone down." He wouldn't take the county's trust for granted. Not this time. He'd been given a second chance to finish his term sober, and with honor. Bishop Harrison had advised him to ease out of the *Englisch* world one step at a time. That's exactly what he planned to do.

Six more months, and I'm done.

"Glad to hear it," Lopez said. "Can't say it's been comfortable filling in for you."

Evan offered a nod. "You did a great job, Diego. And I thank you for that."

Lopez jotted down a few notes. "*De nada*," he murmured in Spanish before reaching for another folder. "Now, about the suspect behind all this trouble…"

"Any leads?"

Lopez's expression hardened. "Still waiting on lab results. Even with Ranger Palmer pushing to speed things up, it could take months. Meanwhile, he'll stay involved and consult with you as the case progresses. Anything that comes up, report it directly to him."

"Understood," Evan replied. While he was all too familiar with the drawn-out waits for blood and DNA evidence, he was grateful for Palmer's continued assistance. With the sheriff's department stretched thin, having a ranger's expertise on hand was a welcome lifeline.

Lopez sighed, the weight of the situation evident. "It's been frustrating, but patience is all we have. When those results come in, we'll have a clearer idea of who we're dealing with."

"I hope it's soon." The memory of that chaotic morning still haunted him, along with the chilling possibility that the town was still under threat.

"So far, no new incidents reported," Lopez added.

The silence wasn't comforting. If anything, it deepened his sense of foreboding.

"The second he reappears, I'll be ready," he said with conviction. "I won't rest until he's behind bars."

"I'm just grateful things are getting back to normal." Standing, Deputy Lopez offered his hand. "Welcome back, Sheriff."

Evan rose, returning the gesture. "Thank you."

Letting his hand drop, Lopez let out a nervous chuckle. "Guess you'll be wanting your office back."

"Don't sweat it." Reaching for his hat, he ran his fingers along the brim before settling it on his head with a familiar motion. "I'll be in Monday morning."

Lopez smiled. "Sounds good."

Exiting his office, Evan paused to take in the familiar sight of the sheriff's department. The air was thick with the aroma of stale coffee and the low buzz of activity.

"Hey, Sheriff! Got a minute?" Andrea Richards waved him over, her voice brightening the dimly lit space.

"What's up?" he asked.

She grinned. "I heard you're coming back."

"That's the plan."

"Good." She wrinkled her nose. "Can't say I've enjoyed working under Lopez. You're the best boss I've had."

"I appreciate that," he said, offering a muted nod.

Her smile dimmed. "Is everything okay? You seem off."

"I don't think I'll be doing this much longer."

"Oh," she said, the surprise clear in her voice. "Why not?"

Evan's gaze drifted away. "I got shot," he said bluntly. "And something like that makes you think hard about what really matters." He looked back to her, his tone roughened by truth. "I'm ready for a different kind of life. Something steady. I'd like to get married, settle down…"

"That sounds wonderful to me." Andrea tilted

her head, studying him with interest. "Got anyone special in mind?"

"Can't say, but I'm hopeful."

"Come on." She leaned in. "Don't keep me guessing. Give me a hint. Who is she?"

Evan shook his head, careful not to overstep decorum. He and Isla weren't official—yet. "The minute she says yes, everyone will know."

"Then I'll cross my fingers she does."

"Thanks." Bidding her a pleasant afternoon, he ended the exchange.

As he turned to go, Andrea gave a light wave. "Oh, I almost forgot. I've got your mail. It's been piling up."

"Thanks for holding it," he said, accepting the stack.

"Have a good weekend, Sheriff." Giving a nod, she turned back to her computer.

Returning the gesture, he headed toward the exit. He paused outside, thumbing through the stack. Bills. Junk. But then his eye caught something different. An envelope heavier than the rest, it was clearly a greeting card.

Curiosity piqued, he tore it open. A birthday card slipped out, innocuous at first glance. But when he unfolded it, his pulse jolted.

You're not getting better, someone had scrawled beneath the cheery greeting. *Just closer to the grave.*

Pulse spiking, he flipped the card over, searching for some clue. Nothing. No signature. No return address. Just his name, address and a postmark indicating it had traveled from the neighboring town.

His hackles rose. If this was meant to be a joke, it was far from funny. His birthday was coming up in a few days, sure. But this felt personal, intentionally cruel.

Just like that note in the cemetery.

Once was an oddity. But two? That was no coincidence. A pattern was emerging, and the picture it painted was one he didn't like.

A thought flashed through his mind, sharp and unsettling. The man who'd shot him hadn't been caught. Was this his way of sending a warning?

Frowning, he shoved the card back into the envelope and headed back into the station. Passing it to Palmer for analysis might yield nothing. But if this was more than a prank, then the threat was still out there.

Watching.

And possibly waiting to strike again.

Isla hummed softly as she smoothed the final layer of icing over the cake, her strokes slow and deliberate. The day was a special one, Evan's thirty-fifth birthday. But it wasn't just another year marked on the calendar; it symbolized a second chance, a step toward healing for a man who had been through so much.

"How's the cake coming?" Leah Miller asked, glancing up from her own task.

"Almost done," she replied, smoothing a few uneven edges. Vanilla with buttercream icing, it wasn't fancy. But it had been made with care, a quiet reflection of the feelings she hadn't yet spoken aloud.

Leah smiled. "The cake looks lovely. You really outdid yourself." A slender, soft-spoken woman with gentle, doe-like eyes, she'd prepared her son's favorite meal: meatloaf and mashed potatoes, accompanied by the comforting trimmings that would turn the simple meal into a feast. Enticing aromas filled the air, wrapping the *haus* in a sense of home and togetherness.

"I'm honored to be invited," Isla said, laying aside the spatula.

"You've always been part of our *familie*," Leah said. "I'm so thankful you're in Evan's life again."

"You two always made a lovely couple," Hazel added. "I'm so happy you're seeing each other again."

Isla's cheeks flushed. "We're not courting," she scoffed, hoping her tone didn't give away the tiny spark of longing that she fought to ignore.

Leah bent, peeking into the oven. "Well, I'm hoping that changes soon." A playful mix of enthusiasm and mischief laced her voice.

Hazel grinned, her own gaze twinkling. "I'm sure it will."

Isla threw up her hands in mock surrender. "Please, we're taking things one day at a time," she insisted, trying to sound more practical than she felt. "Just like the Lord tells us to."

"Might be that the Lord's telling you something else," Leah said, carefully placing the hot pan on the countertop. "I'll pray that we both have the same thing in mind."

Isla's heart skipped. She looked down, trying to hide her smile. After so long guarding her heart, could this be what she'd prayed for?

Hope stirred quietly inside her.

"We'll see," she said, turning back to her task.

Done with the cake, she covered it with a glass dome. Carrying the bowl and spatula to the sink, she caught a glimpse of the activity outside. Tables and chairs had already been set up beneath a shaded canopy. Joel and Olivia helped with the decorations, their small hands tying balloons and streamers that fluttered in the gentle breeze. Everyone was eager to contribute to the surprise party.

She smiled at the sight. Getting Evan out for the afternoon had taken careful planning. Jonah had set it all in motion, asking for help to remove some stubborn tree stumps. Always willing to lend a hand, Evan had agreed without much fuss. Unaware of the true purpose behind the request, he'd taken his vehicle to help. Later, the men would return to Hazel's for supper and the party that awaited. Having put aside their differences, the Millers were attempting to come together and support each other.

Isla washed the dishes and stacked them to dry. Happy as she was about the day ahead, a sense of foreboding cast a shadow over her thoughts. Evan had been cleared by both his physicians and was scheduled to go back to work. His sense of responsibility, his commitment to the community, wouldn't allow him to simply walk away.

Shaking her head, she blew out a breath. *It's just like him to do that.* He was stubborn, principled and unyielding. She admired that about him, though she couldn't help but worry. His steadfastness was admirable, but it also carried a price.

Despite the uncertainty, she found comfort in knowing this part of Evan's life was almost over. Once he'd fulfilled his obligations, he could retire. He'd promised he would, and she believed him.

With a soft sigh, she turned her gaze heavenward. *Lord, keep him safe, please.*

Joel and Olivia burst back into the kitchen, their excited giggles filling the air. Hambone trotted behind, snorting with curiosity. Stewart skittered along at their heels, his ringed tail swishing.

"What can we do now?" Joel asked, bouncing on his toes, his enthusiasm barely contained.

Hazel reached into a cabinet, taking down a large glass bowl. "How about you two help me with the party punch?"

"Can we?" Olivia chirped, clapping her hands.

"Certainly," Hazel said, moving toward the counter where the ingredients waited to be mixed.

Working under close supervision, the children combined fresh orange juice and sweet grape juice, before adding a splash of lemon for tang. As Joel stirred it all together, Olivia added a bottle of ginger ale, which gave the punch a bubbly lift. The mixture was then poured over sliced strawberries. Later it would be ladled over glasses filled to the brim with ice.

"Perfect," Hazel declared, giving the *youngies* her enthusiastic approval.

Determined not to be ignored, Hambone nudged in, looking for a bite. Stewart lifted on his hind legs, drawn by the promise of something to eat.

Olivia couldn't contain her giggles. "Not for critters," she exclaimed as she waved a finger playfully at the two hopeful beggars.

Hazel chuckled. "Let them have the leftover fruit."

Joel carefully selected a few berries. "Here's some." He held them out, his small hands steady and confident.

Hambone snuffled up the treat with gusto. Stewart grabbed his share, clutching the fruit in his paws and nibbling happily.

Laughing, Leah shook her head. "Oh, Hazel, you spoil them so."

The old lady gave her cherished pets a fond look. "They're *familie*, too."

The lighthearted moment was abruptly shattered by a sudden, sharp bang that rattled the front door. The force of it startled Isla. It wasn't the knock of someone arriving for a celebration. It was more insistent, almost as if the person on the other side was determined not to be ignored.

Hazel looked up, her brow furrowing with concern. "Who could that be?"

As if expecting the worst, Leah's face drained of color. "Please, *Gott*, no," she murmured.

Isla glanced between the two women, her chest tightening with unease. "I'm sure it's nothing." Even to her own ears, her voice sounded hollow, lacking conviction.

The banging came again. Harder. More insistent.

No one moved. No one dared to break the heavy dread that enveloped them.

"I'll get it." Smoothing the wrinkles out of her apron, Isla moved toward the door. With each step, her apprehension grew, but she opened to the demanding visitor.

A man wearing a poorly fitted suit stood on the porch. His complexion was pallid, drawn tight over angular bones. His deep-set eyes, hollowed by dark circles, flickered with an unsettling intensity beneath his wide brow. Clutching a small box wrapped in plain brown paper, his demeanor betrayed a nervous energy.

"Can I help you?" she asked, attempting to remain composed.

The stranger's gaze flicked up to meet hers. "Sheriff Miller live here?"

Isla took an involuntary step back. There was something about his presence that unsettled her. Despite the weakness that clung to him, she couldn't shake the uneasy feeling that something about him was very dangerous.

"Why do you want to know?"

"Because I got something for him," the stranger said, extending his offering. The movement briefly bared his wrist, revealing a tattoo.

Isla hesitated. The man's presence, the way he carried himself, all felt wrong. Deeply wrong. But not wanting to appear rude, she accepted his offering.

"I'll make sure he gets it," she said. "Shall I tell him who it's from?"

The stranger's lips curled. "Oh, he'll know." Without waiting for a reply, he pivoted and walked away, the subtle limp in his step betraying the source of his discomfort.

Reaching the gate, he pushed it open and continued toward a sleek gray vehicle parked at the end of the drive. Windows tinted, the car sat tucked away as if the stranger had gone to lengths to keep his presence unnoticed. When he reached the driver's side, he paused to look back.

Isla's gut twisted. She felt the prickling awareness of the man's gaze, a predator's scrutiny that made her skin crawl. His eyes narrowed, as if he were assessing every inch of the house and its vulnerabilities.

A long minute passed, and then another.

Finally, the unwelcome visitor slid into his vehicle, shutting the door with a hollow thud. The sedan roared to life, pulling away with a spray of dirt and gravel.

Clutching the box, Isla quickly closed the door and locked it. There was something unsettling about the man's actions, something menacing. Hands trembling slightly, she examined the package.

What should I do?

Hazel approached. "Who was that?"

Isla hesitated, a strange unease creeping over her. "I didn't recognize him," she said, shivering. "But I'm glad he's gone. He didn't seem friendly."

Hazel glanced at the package. "Did he bring that?"

"He asked me to make sure Evan got it."

Glancing toward the kitchen, Hazel lifted a single finger, an indication not to alarm the others. "Best to give it to him later," she mouthed. "When the others aren't around."

"I will," Isla said, placing the parcel out of sight.

The rest of the afternoon slipped by in a blur. Before long, the front door opened again. This time Evan stepped inside, oblivious to the surprise waiting for him. His father and brothers all followed him in.

"*Gute gubbotta dawg*!" The room erupted, voices loud and filled with joy.

Evan grinned at the sight. "What in the world?"

Leah rushed forward, pulling him into a hug. "Did you really think we'd let your birthday go by without a fuss?"

Evan chuckled, shaking his head as he hugged his mother back. "I didn't expect this at all."

Everyone crowded around, offering hugs, handshakes and playful teasing as they led him outside to the backyard, set up and ready for the evening's celebration.

Isla lingered behind, her thoughts resting on the stranger and his odd delivery. As much as she wanted to stay in the warmth of the celebration, the creeping sense of unease refused to leave her.

Something's not right.

Evan stepped back through the screen door. "I hope you're planning to join us."

Isla waved him inside. "Actually, something arrived for you," she said, hurrying to retrieve the package. "I don't mean to ruin the moment, but I think you should look at this."

"What is it?"

"A man left it earlier today."

"Oh? Who?"

"I've never seen him before," she said. "But he seemed to know you."

A shadow passed over Evan's face, apprehension sparking in his eyes. "Wonder who it was?" His gaze lingered on the unmarked brown paper as if it might hold answers. Slowly, he began to peel away the wrapping.

Isla held out a hand. "Wait—don't open it." Fear squeezed hard, threatening to cut off her air. She didn't know how to explain, but the certainty within her couldn't be shaken. "I don't think that came from a *freund*." She wanted to say more but couldn't find the right words to make him understand. He hadn't seen the man who'd delivered the package.

But she had.

And the emotionless malice in the stranger's eyes was something born of pure evil.

Chapter Thirteen

The strange gift had arrived like a whisper in the noise, but as it didn't seem dangerous, Evan decided to let the party play out. Everyone had gone through a lot of trouble to give him a memorable day. Why ruin it?

The festivities continued, laughter bubbling through the air, kids and pets darting between the adults. His parents were in high spirits, his mamm gushing over the dessert table while his *daed* told the same old stories that made everyone laugh. His brothers were even louder, teasing Evan about getting older and slower. But beneath the joviality, Evan felt a subtle, gnawing tension that he couldn't quite shake.

He played the part well, smiling and nodding, concealing his unease behind the veneer of a birthday celebration. Isla, too, wore her mask, her demeanor calm, though he could sense the quiet solidarity in her gaze. They both knew something was off, but neither mentioned it. Not yet.

It wasn't until the last hugs were exchanged, the

buggy carrying his family slowly pulling away, that the tension in Evan's chest finally started to loosen.

He turned to Isla, keeping his voice low. "Time to deal with this."

Casting a glance toward Hazel and the children, she nodded.

Ready to act, Evan pulled out his phone and dialed Glen Palmer.

The ranger arrived an hour later—and he wasn't alone. Expecting trouble, he'd brought a hazardous devices expert. The specialist moved with quiet precision, carefully retrieving the box from the shed where Evan had discreetly stashed it. Better safe than sorry.

Tense minutes passed.

Finally, expert returned, his expression unreadable. "It's not a bomb," he said. "It's a message." He opened the box to reveal a toy-sized coffin. Inside lay a single artificial yellow daisy, silk petals still and perfect. A note was tied to the stem in looping, deliberate handwriting.

Soon you'll be pushing up daisies.

A chill crept up Evan's spine. "No mistaking that one."

"Tag it and bag it," Palmer said, motioning for the agent to secure the evidence. Arms folded across his chest, he turned back to Evan. "You've got an enemy."

"No doubt." Except for Palmer, no one else

knew about the earlier notes he'd received. But now a vital line had been crossed. His stalker knew where he lived and was growing bolder. And, possibly, more dangerous.

"I don't like where this is headed," Palmer said. "Can you tell me how it got here, and when?"

"I was out," he explained. "Isla is the one who answered the door. She had the closest contact with the suspect."

"I'm going to have to talk to her."

Evan cast a glance toward the living room, where Isla sat, her face pale but her posture remarkably composed. Despite the tension in the air, she'd continued to hold herself together with a quiet strength.

"I know." Leaning in, he lowered his voice. "Go easy, okay? She's not used to this kind of thing."

"I'll be as gentle as I can," Palmer promised.

"Thank you."

Together, the two men stepped into the living room, the silence pressing in around them.

Hands clasped, Isla sat perched on the sofa. To keep Joel and Olivia distanced from the matter, Hazel had discreetly ushered the children outside, murmuring something about putting away the leftovers. The gesture was meant to shield them from the gravity of the conversation, giving the adults privacy to speak.

"Evening, Mrs. Bruhn," Palmer said, tipping his head. "I hope you don't mind, but I need to ask you a few questions."

Isla's gaze lifted. "I'll do anything I can to help."

"I understand you were the one who took the delivery." Palmer's tone was gentle but authoritative. "Can you tell me about the man who delivered it?"

"He knocked while we were cooking. When I opened the door, he stated he had something for the sheriff. He asked me to give it to him."

"Can you describe him?" Palmer asked.

"He was tall…maybe six feet. His hair was blond, messy, like he hadn't combed it in a while." She hesitated, her fingers worrying the edges of her apron.

"That's all very helpful," Palmer said, nodding thoughtfully. "Was there anything else that caught your attention?"

"He wore *Englisch* clothes. But they didn't fit. He was pale, too, like he'd been ill. There was a tattoo on his wrist, too."

Palmer's gaze sharpened. "Could you tell what it was?"

"A snake coiled around a dagger." Pausing, she scrunched up her face. "And he walked with a limp."

Evan tensed as he listened intently to the exchange. He couldn't help but admire the way Isla had kept her cool. She didn't deserve to be caught in this web of danger, but here she was, facing it head-on.

The questions continued. "Did you see what he was driving?"

"*Ja*. A gray automobile."

"Did you see the model or license plate?" Palmer asked, eager for more information.

Isla expression blanked. "I—didn't."

"That's okay, Mrs. Bruhn," Palmer said. "What you've given me is very helpful. Thank you."

Isla visibly shivered. "I wish I could forget the sight of him."

The ranger gave Evan a look. "Anyone you know?"

Evan ran a hand through his hair as his mind churned through faces and names. After years on the job, sorting through a roster of the angry and disgruntled was like flipping through a well-worn book. Arrests rarely left people feeling grateful. He'd had his share of threats from folks who weren't happy to be slapped in cuffs.

"Honestly, I've locked up plenty of men who weren't happy to go to jail. But it's hard to say who's angry enough to take things this far."

"Maybe I can help narrow it down." Without waiting for a response, Palmer strode over to the side table where he'd left his briefcase.

Evan tensed. Something told him Palmer was already ten steps ahead.

Palmer opened the briefcase, revealing an interior filled with neatly organized folders. "When I got your call," he began, glancing back with an expression that blended concern and determination, "something occurred to me. Thought I'd bring this along just in case."

"And?"

Palmer extracted a manila folder, its worn edges hinting at previous use. Walking back to Isla, he flipped it open with a smooth motion, revealing a black-and-white photo tucked inside.

"Does he look familiar?"

Isla leaned forward. Recognition washed over her, draining the color from her face. "*Ja*. That's the man."

Evan looked, too. "Who is it?"

Palmer turned the mugshot around. "Happens to be the lowlife thug who shot you," the ranger drawled. "His name is Sammy Lazzaro. The DNA results came in just a few hours ago, matter of fact. Haven't really had time to go over it, but here we are."

"Never heard of him."

"Sammy's a small-time thief," Palmer replied. "He usually sticks to quick holdups, in-and-out robberies where he can get cash fast. They call him 'the Snatch' because he can't keep his hands off other people's property."

"Go on."

"Normally, Sammy's the kind who avoids confrontation. But if he was willing to pull a gun on a cop, something's changed."

"Lot of felons get tired of the return trip."

"He's been in the system since he was a juvenile, always getting early release because he's a good boy behind bars," Palmer said. "Guys like Sammy get trapped in a vicious cycle; prison, release, back to the streets, then right back behind bars. At some point, they'll do whatever it takes to break free of it. He violated his parole and disappeared off the grid last year."

That made sense. Unwilling to return to the pen, Sammy Lazzaro had lashed out at law enforcement to avoid capture.

I just happened to be the one in his way.

"Looks like we've got a fugitive on our hands," he said. "So why not leave town while the going is good?"

Palmer shifted the folder in his hands, tapping it thoughtfully. His gaze flicked toward Isla. "You mentioned he walked with a limp, correct?"

"*Ja,*" she affirmed. "He was perspiring like he was in pain."

"I'd bet my last dollar Sammy's been holed up right under our noses, nursing his wound from the shootout. A bum leg means no more fast escapes. Career's dead in the water."

Evan felt a chill circle his spine. The import of Palmer's speculation settled like a stone in his gut. "You think he's decided to get even?"

"Apparently," Palmer replied dryly. "If Sammy's bold enough to walk up to your front door, there's nothing stopping him from trying to finish what he started."

Evan exhaled slowly, the seriousness of the situation settling on his shoulders. Taken on their own, the notes hadn't seemed that threatening. Tasteless, yes, but otherwise seemingly harmless. But now that they had a name and a face behind the threats, vigilance wasn't enough.

His thoughts flickered to the people he loved most. The last thing he wanted was for them to become collateral in whatever mess he was stepping into. The threat wasn't just against him anymore. It was against everything he'd worked to protect.

"That isn't going to happen," he said. "I'll assign a deputy to watch the property."

"I've got extra men if you need them," Palmer offered. "Just say the word, and they'll be here."

Evan gave a short nod. His department was stretched too thin to manage round-the-clock coverage. "I'll take whatever help you can spare."

"It's on the way." Retrieving his briefcase, the older man tucked away his folder.

"Sounds good."

"The sooner we alert the public, the better," Palmer continued. "Citizens are our best eyes and ears at this point. I'll ensure the details are released to the press immediately. There's no doubt that Lazzaro is dangerous. We need to get him off the streets, pronto."

"I agree." Even as he spoke, Evan's thoughts

were already on the manhunt. Every additional cop on the street would bring them one step closer to apprehending the fugitive.

"I'll get things in motion." Briefcase in hand, Palmer strode toward the door, his footsteps echoing softly in the quiet room. "Don't hesitate to call if you need anything." The ranger exited, the door clicking shut behind him.

A long silence settled, heavy with things unspoken.

Evan looked to Isla, trying to gauge her mood. Her expression was tight, shadowed with an emotion he couldn't quite read. But the tension in the air between them spoke volumes.

"It's fine," he insisted. "Everything's under control."

Isla didn't blink. "That's not true, and you know it."

"You're right," he admitted. "But it's nothing that involves you."

She didn't respond immediately. When she did, her voice trembled. "I'm already involved."

Torn between the need to shield her and the grim reality closing in, he curled his hands into fists. "No, you're not," he insisted, his tone sharper then intended. "You and the kids are going home. Right now."

A flash of hurt flickered in her gaze. "You're sending us away?"

Evan nodded, the weight of the decision dragging at him. "It's the only way I know to keep you safe. Until I catch up with Lazarro, you don't need to be anywhere near me."

"Why does it have to be you?" she demanded. "That man almost killed you. Why not let Palmer take it from here?"

He hesitated. "I could. But if this ends badly... I want it on me."

"Even if it means dying?" she flung back.

"Yes."

A visible tremor ran through her. "I don't know if I could survive that," she whispered. "Losing you... again."

Evan couldn't reply.

For a long moment, they stood in the quiet shadow between what they wanted and what the world demanded of them.

And then, with a slow, reluctant nod, Isla stepped back. Her message was unmistakable. She was releasing her hold. On him. On hope. On what they'd almost had.

Her surrender shredded Evan inside, leaving him raw and bereft. He ached to reach for her, to promise her the future they'd dreamed of. But right now, he had no future to offer.

Not with a target on his back.

Swallowing the pain, he let his gaze drift to the cabinet where his service revolver lay locked away. Whatever it took, he'd protect Isla and the children.

Even if it meant losing everything.

* * *

As Isla absentmindedly cleaned the kitchen, her thoughts were miles away, caught in the same loop they'd been trapped in for days.

Evan had gone back to work.

A week had passed since they'd last spoken and his absence from her life weighed on her. She'd prayed that his return to the Amish community would be an easy transition, that he would be able to leave his turbulent past behind. But that hope had all but evaporated.

Isla tried to understand. She really did. Evan's commitment to his job ran deep, too deep for him to find peace while Sammy Lazzaro was still at large. While that man was out there, everyone was at risk. The local paper had recently published updates, confirming the fugitive was the mastermind behind the string of robberies terrorizing the area. Law enforcement urged residents to report any sighting of the criminal. But Lazzaro had vanished again, and the uncertainty of his whereabouts gnawed at everyone.

Evan's position wasn't easy. He'd sworn to protect his community, and he took that vow seriously. But this had gone beyond responsibility. Sammy Lazarro had made it clear he intended to kill the lawman.

Keeping her at arm's length wasn't a rejection. It was Evan's way of shielding her, of standing between her and the danger that stalked his steps.

How can I fault him for that?

Still, even understanding the why didn't make it hurt any less. The future they might have shared hovered just out of her reach like sunlight on water, shimmering and beautiful, but impossible to hold.

Isla sighed, aching with the weight of longing. She couldn't ask Evan to be less than he was. Not even for her.

But that didn't mean it didn't hurt.

The creak of the floor behind her caught her attention.

"*Mamm*, is Sheriff Miller coming today?" Joel asked.

Pausing, Isla brushed a lock of stray hair out of her eyes. "*Nein*, he's not. Why?"

Joel glanced at the ball in his hand. "I was hoping he might come and play with me again."

Isla gave him a sorrowful glance. Her *sohn* had grown attached to Evan so quickly. "I don't think he has the time."

That, she believed, was true enough. Now and then, she caught a glimpse of his black SUV prowling the neighborhood, but that was all. Deputies also stopped by several times a day, their holstered weapons in plain view. The sight unsettled her more than she liked to admit. Still, their presence offered a measure of reassurance.

For the moment, things felt almost normal.

Almost.

"But he used to come, almost every day," Joel said sadly.

"I know you miss him. I miss him, too," she said, smoothing his bangs off his forehead. "But you must understand, the sheriff has important work to do. He's keeping everyone safe from bad people."

His youthful brow knitted. "Like the man who took our money?"

"*Ja*. The sheriff will catch him, so he can be punished for what he did."

"But what if he can't?" Joel's voice wavered, his fears bubbling up. "What if the bad guy hurts him again?"

"The sheriff is very strong. He knows how to take care of himself. He's been doing this for a long time."

"Do you think he misses us?" Joel asked, his innocence cutting through her thoughts.

"I'm sure he does," she replied, though doubt flickered in her mind. The ache of Evan's absence loomed larger, and she wondered if he could ever find his way back to them, or if he even wanted to. "Why don't you ask Olivia to play?"

Joel sighed, a hint of disappointment in his voice. "I already asked her, but she said she doesn't want to."

She forced a smile. "Once I'm finished cleaning up, we can go to the park." It wasn't Olivia's fault. Her daughter was outgrowing the carefree days of childhood. She preferred spending time with her friends, discussing cute *boi*s and sharing secrets.

Joel brightened at the mention. "Really? Can we go soon?"

"Of course, sweetie. Just a little longer."

Pushing away the sadness that had settled in her chest, Isla returned to her cleaning. Life had to go on, even without Evan. She had to be strong. For her children, and herself.

The rest of the day unfolded through the long afternoon. Returning from the park, they made dinner together. Olivia kneaded the bread, while Joel peeled potatoes and carrots. As they worked side by side, the kitchen filled with the comforting sounds of clinking pots and sizzling ingredients.

After supper, Isla sent the children to their rooms to study. Her work beckoned.

With careful precision, she began stitching a delicate hem on a dress, the rhythmic motion of the needle bringing a sense of calm. The thread slipped through her fingers, and she poured her heart into the garment.

All in all, they were carrying on with their lives, a small, tight-knit family finding joy in the simplest of moments.

A sudden noise snapped Isla out of her task. Pausing, she listened, straining to catch the sound again. It was faint, a rustling. Someone was walking around outside.

Laying aside the dress, she rose from her sewing table. She crept toward the bay windows, peering out into the darkness. Nothing seemed out of place, but the uneasy feeling in her chest wouldn't go away.

And then she saw it. A dark figure moving across the porch, lurking in the shadowy space. The intruder paused. A spark came to light.

Her breath caught. *What's happening?*

Before she could think twice, something crashed through the window with a loud shatter. A glass bottle, flaming at the top, landed on the floor with a sickening thud. Flames exploded outward, licking at the carpet and spreading across the floor.

The intruder fled, disappearing through the front gate. A flash of taillights and the squeal of tires followed.

Inhaling the acrid scent of gasoline, Isla's heart thundered in her chest. The fire threatened to consume everything in its path.

No, no, no!

Panic surged through her veins, propelling her toward the inferno. Her hands trembled as she snatched a thick blanket, her mind racing as she tried to smother the flames. But the heat was overwhelming, the fire was too fierce, too relentless. It devoured everything in its path.

The children were still upstairs.

"Joel! Olivia!" she screamed, her voice cracking under the strain of her terror as she darted out of the living room.

"Mamm!" Joel's frightened voice echoed from the top of the stairs. Both children stood wide-eyed and terrified, confusion etched on their faces.

"What's happening?" Olivia cried.

"Run! Get outside!" Isla shouted. The heat was unbearable, a suffocating wave that threatened to engulf her. Smoke billowed, stinging her eyes and choking her lungs.

"I've got to get Mittens!" Olivia wailed, fear morphing into a frantic cry as she turned to race back toward her room for her cat.

"Olivia, no!" Isla screamed, fear surging through her veins. "Come on!" she urged, panic rising.

Olivia emerged, clutching her beloved pet. "I've got her," she cried, rushing down the stairs with Joel following behind.

They burst outside into the cool night air, the sudden chill contrasting sharply with the heat radiating from the inferno behind them. Flames roared, sending fiery sparks into the sky.

The world outside transformed into a chaotic blur as the flames erupted, crackling and roaring, reaching toward the night sky. Neighbors surged forward, their faces flickering in the orange glow of the fire, eyes wide with fear and disbelief. Shouts intertwined, creating a frantic symphony of alarm and urgency that pierced through the night as the fire raged higher, engulfing the house in a consuming embrace.

"What happened?" Abner Pilcher shouted, his voice a mix of panic and urgency as he sprinted across the street.

Verna followed in his wake, her eyes wide. "*Gott* save us all!"

Isla stood frozen. The acrid smell of smoke invaded her senses, stinging her eyes and throat as she struggled to comprehend the horrifying scene unfolding before her. The familiar, comforting space filled with laughter, warmth and cherished memories was now a chaotic blaze.

"Someone threw something through the front window," she babbled. "It just burst into flames—" The story tumbled out in a breathless rush, but it felt woefully inadequate to capture the sheer disbelief of that moment. The crack of the glass shattering echoed in her mind, a prelude to the fiery explosion that followed.

The distant wail of sirens pierced the air, growing louder as fire trucks roared onto the scene, their bright lights flashing. A patrol unit followed close behind, the SUV's blue-and-red lights casting an otherworldly glow on the faces of terrified onlookers, their expressions a mix of concern and helplessness. As firefighters sprang into action, dragging heavy hoses from the trucks and shouting commands to one another, a familiar figure emerged from the throng.

Evan moved with purpose, cutting through the chaos with calm authority.

Isla barely had time to process his arrival before he swept her into his arms. His embrace was firm yet gentle.

"Stay close," he instructed, guiding her away from the blaze.

"The children—" she gasped. "Joel... Olivia..."

"They're with Verna," Abner said, pointing toward the cluster of fire trucks, where Joel and Olivia stood, clinging to each other. Their faces were pale, their bodies trembling with cold and fear, tears streaking down their cheeks.

"Come on!" Evan commanded, propelling her to safety.

Isla rushed to her children, enveloping them in her arms. "It's okay, I'm here."

"*Mamm*," Joel cried, bursting into panicked sobs. "I don't understand what's happening..."

"I'm scared!" Olivia whimpered.

Isla cradled her *kinder* closer, sending up a silent prayer. *Thank You, Gott, that we're safe*.

They had gotten out alive, and that was all that mattered.

Staring at the remnants of her house, the weight of loss sank in, crashing down on her with an unrelenting force.

Everything she owned was gone.

Chapter Fourteen

Isla cupped her hands under the water, splashing it onto her face. The soot and grime from the fire clung stubbornly to her skin, and she scrubbed harder, watching the dark streaks swirl down the drain. The blaze had stolen everything; her home, her possessions and any sense of safety she'd had left. As she stood there, trembling, she felt it all crumbling down around her. The fire might be out, but the fear still smoldered inside her.

Thankfully, everyone was safe. Now, the *kinder* were tucked into bed in one of Hazel's spare rooms. For tonight, they had a roof over their heads. But tomorrow, they'd wake up to the reality of their loss. And she wasn't sure how to be strong enough for all of them.

Turning off the faucet, Isla grabbed a towel and pressed it to her face. When she finally looked into the mirror, she hardly recognized the woman staring back. Her skin was pale, and her eyes were wide, hollow with exhaustion and grief.

Why had this happened?

Trembling, Isla willed herself not to fall apart. To allay the fear, she forced herself to take slow, deep breaths, focusing on the Lord's many promises of safety and divine protection.

Yea, though I walk through the valley of the shadow of death, I will fear no evil...

The familiar prayer helped calm her, bringing her pulse back to a normal rhythm. Given time, their material possessions could all be replaced. What mattered most was that they had been spared, protected by a force far greater than themselves. She did not doubt that *Gott*'s hand had guided them to safety.

She draped the damp towel over the rack to dry. She covered the borrowed cotton nightdress with a long, fluffy blue robe. The slippers Hazel had loaned her offered protection against the cold floor. As she pinned her damp hair into a gentle twist at the nape of her neck, a soft knock came at the door.

"It's me, dear," Hazel called. "I just wanted to make sure you have everything you need."

Isla hesitated, composing herself before opening the door. "*Ja*, I'm fine," she said, stepping into the hallway. "I appreciate everything you've done."

"I'm just thankful everyone is safe."

"I can't begin to express how grateful I am," she said. "We had no other place to go."

"This *haus* has more than enough room." Hazel's lips pressed together, forming a thin line. "I don't see much of Evan since he's gone back to work. He's gone almost all day and night. Only comes home to sleep."

Isla's heart pinched at the thought of Evan pushing himself to the brink. He'd always been that way. His absence in their lives had left a small, aching void. Not that it should matter. He'd made his choice to keep working, distancing himself from the community and from her.

But still…

She refocused, pushing the unwanted thoughts away. "I'm glad he's out there, doing what he does," she confessed.

Gripped by terror, she'd been too panicked to think clearly, her mind blank with shock. Burr Oak's sheriff had appeared, stepping into the bedlam with calm certainty. Evan had taken charge with an authority that left no room for doubt, guiding her and the children away from the collapsing structure while helping coordinate the volunteer firefighters scrambling to douse the flames. His hand was firm on her shoulder, grounding her, giving her something solid to focus on when everything else felt like it was slipping away.

Attempting to clear away the persistent ache, Isla shook her head. She didn't want to feel this way—to be grateful, or to be so affected by him. But it was impossible not to remember the way he'd pulled her close, if only for a few seconds.

She'd felt safe, even if she knew it was fleeting. Even if she knew he would leave again.

He always did.

Whatever had existed between them was in the past. He'd chosen his path, and she had hers. She had her children to think about, and the aftermath of the fire to deal with. There was no room in her life for impossible dreams.

"*Gott* was with you," Hazel said. "I've made some chamomile tea. Why don't you come down and have a cup? It might help you relax."

"That would be nice." There was no way she'd sleep. Not tonight. "I'll be down after I check on the children."

"Come when you're ready," Hazel said.

Isla continued down the hallway. Reaching one of the guest rooms, she pushed the door open, making sure not to disturb the precious quiet. The space was dimly lit, and she could just make out two peaceful forms. Joel's tousled hair stuck up in all directions, his chest rising and falling in a steady rhythm, while Olivia slept curled up with a quilt pulled beneath her chin. The hour had been late when they'd tumbled into bed, exhausted.

A soft sigh escaped as she watched them. The *youngies* had been through so much already. Losing their father, the robbery, the fire… And yet, they were resilient. Stronger than she often gave them credit for. With everything still so uncertain, they needed that strength more than ever.

"Lord, keep them safe," she murmured.

With one last look, Isla pulled the door closed. She padded down the staircase and into the living room. The soft glow of lamps throughout guided her toward the kitchen. The calming scent of chamomile and mint filled the air.

She found Hazel waiting at the table, her hands cradling a steaming mug of tea. Across the room, Evan stood looking out the window. Though Hambone and Stewart were nowhere to be found, Hazel's big yellow tomcat lounged nearby, regarding them all through narrow eyes.

"Come, sit," the old lady beckoned, patting the chair near hers. "You must be exhausted."

Moving on autopilot, Isla slid into the chair.

Hazel rose, hurrying to the kettle on the stove. "How are the children?" she asked, filling a mug to the brim before placing it on the table.

Isla gratefully accepted the drink. The heat seeped into her hands, but she didn't bring it to her lips right away. "They're sleeping, finally."

"I'm happy they're resting," Hazel said, placing a hand on her shoulder.

Isla's gaze drifted to the strong but silent figure by the window. Evan looked tense, his shoulders rigid beneath his shirt. She knew that look. He was frustrated, and angry.

"Thank you for being there tonight," Isla said to Evan. "We couldn't have managed without you."

"I didn't do enough," he snapped back. "If I'd

been doing my job, you wouldn't be sitting here, homeless, because I failed to protect you."

Isla flinched at the bitterness in his tone. "That's not true. You saved us. We're here because of you." Shifting into action, he'd moved swiftly to take them into protective custody, pulling her and the children from the danger and transporting them to the sheriff's office. Glen Palmer had been on-site, and his inquiry had dragged on for what felt like hours. By the end of her eyewitness account, there was no doubt in anyone's mind. The fire wasn't an accident. It was deliberate.

One name kept coming up: the specter of the man who haunted her nightmares—Sammy Lazzaro. The man who'd robbed her home was now the prime suspect in the arson.

The knowledge sent a fresh wave of dread crashing over her. Lazzaro was dangerous, a felon with a violent past. She'd seen firsthand the havoc he'd wreaked. But why come after her and the children?

"I don't understand why this is happening," she finished, again close to tears.

Scaling back his attitude, Evan dragged a hand over his stubbled face. "You didn't do anything. Palmer thinks Lazzaro is trying to get to me through people I care about. He won't take on a man who is armed and ready, so he went after those he thinks are vulnerable."

"But the children… They could've been hurt… or worse. How can someone be so heartless?"

"I think he's desperate and knows we're closing in." Grim resolve shadowed every line in his face. "I won't rest until I find him."

"What do we do until then?" Her voice cracked, revealing the fragility she felt inside. "We have no home, no place to go."

Hazel reached out, enveloping Isla's trembling hand within her own warm grasp. "You'll always have a home with us."

"Palmer and I believe it's best if you agree to protective custody," Evan affirmed. "You'll be staying here. And when I'm not present, someone else will be."

Isla swallowed, the lump in her throat making it difficult to speak. "I didn't mean to cause any trouble."

"You're the victim," he countered.

"*Gott* willing, we'll get through this together," Hazel added.

"This will be taken care of," he continued. "It's not a matter of *if* we'll catch him. It's only a matter of *when*." There was something in the way he said it, a firmness that spoke of experience, of battles fought and won.

Isla's head spun. It was all too much to take in at once.

Part of her wanted to believe him, to cling to the hope that the authorities could make everything right. But deep down, she knew how dangerous a criminal on the run was. People like

Lazzaro didn't just disappear. They left scars, destroying everything they touched. The reality of her situation forced her to confront a painful truth: she'd do anything to keep her young ones safe, even if that meant accepting protection from men who carried firearms.

The crackle of Evan's comm link sliced through the tense moment. Stepping aside, he listened to the incoming communication from the dispatcher. Each broken phrase was delivered in sharp, disjointed fragments.

Isla tipped her head, straining to understand the complicated code police spoke in. She understood nothing. Evan's stance tensed as he listened, his shoulders rigid.

Seconds stretched into an eternity.

"Ten-four," he said, finally ending the communication.

Hazel wrung her hands with worry. "What's going on?"

A flash of frustration darkened Evan's expression. "They found Lazzaro."

Isla's pulse stalled. "And?"

"He's dead."

The abandoned gas station loomed on the outskirts of town, its broken windows and faded signage speaking of years of neglect. The faint hum of the wind whistling through the metal beams was the only sound apart from the distant chirping of crickets.

Stepping out of his SUV, Evan tugged his jacket tighter against the chill that settled into his bones, but it wasn't just the uneasy feeling that made him shiver. It was the sight of the gray sedan parked under the station's awning, headlights still casting a dim glow onto the cracked pavement.

A prickling sense of recognition washed over him. It was the same vehicle Isla had described the day Lazarro delivered his macabre gift.

The flash of blue-and-red lights bathed the scene in an eerie glow, but it did little to soften the grimness of what lay before him. Just ahead, Glen Palmer and Deputy Lopez walked around the perimeter of the sedan with slow, deliberate strides.

Flashlight in hand, Evan approached. "What's going on?"

"Lopez found him," Palmer said, skipping the greeting.

Evan shone his light into the car. His stomach turned at the sight before him. The driver was slumped over the wheel, still and silent. A firearm rested loosely in the man's right hand, and a spent casing sat on the passenger seat. The faint scent of smoke lingered in the air, sharp and unsettling. It all pointed to a heartbreaking self-inflicted end.

Sickened by the sight, he stepped back. "Tragic."

"The car matches the description of the one he was last seen driving," Palmer said. "I ran the VIN. It was jacked about six months ago in Dallas. Plates are stolen, too." Walking around to the back, he indicated the trunk. "Looks like he was a busy fella tonight. Got a can of fuel here. Glass bottles and rags, too."

Evan surveyed the scene. All the evidence was there, right in plain sight. It was almost too perfect. Like someone wanted the cops to find it.

"You think he really killed himself?" Lopez asked.

Palmer frowned, stepping closer to the car and peering inside. "Looks clear enough to me. He probably knew he'd crossed the line and couldn't take the heat."

Evan's gaze drifted back to the lifeless perp. The gun was in Lazzaro's hand, but something about the positioning seemed off.

Palmer noticed his hesitation. "What's on your mind?"

Evan scanned the area as if the answers might be hiding in the shadows. This gas station near the intersection leading to the interstate had been abandoned for years. Windows boarded over, the graffiti-covered building was derelict.

"Lazzaro doesn't strike me as the type to go out like this," he said. "He was willing to shoot his way out the last time we got close."

Palmer let out a heavy sigh, rubbing the back of his neck. "Sometimes a man knows when he's reached the point of no return. An autopsy will tell us more, but from where I'm standing, it looks open and shut."

Evan frowned. "It all feels too convenient. Like it's exactly what someone wanted us to find."

"I get that you're not convinced," the ranger went on, his tone steady. "But Lazarro's face was plastered everywhere. We knew exactly who we were after."

"Yeah, but why attack Isla? She did nothing to deserve that."

Palmer shrugged. "Get mad, get even. He couldn't get to you, so he went after her."

That was a no-brainer. Despite the fact Palmer was right, something deep in his gut wouldn't settle.

Questions gnawed at him, but the answers continued to hover just out of his reach. The fact Palmer viewed the incident as straightforward probably meant the case was going to be considered closed. The press outlets would report the details, and the cops would all walk away as heroes.

Evan couldn't shake the feeling they were overlooking vital details.

This isn't right.

Palmer clapped him on the shoulder, jarring him from his thoughts. "Listen, you've been through enough with this case. The whole town has. But it's over. The CSI team is on the way, and we'll get all the details from the autopsy soon."

"Go home and get some rest," Lopez urged. "You look like you could use it."

He gave a tired nod, exhaling slowly. "At least the town can sleep easier tonight."

"Amen to that," Palmer agreed, his tone casual but thoughtful.

Evan started to walk away, then paused. He turned back to the two men, voice steady. "Just so you know, I'm done."

Surprise creased Palmer's brow. "Is that right?"

"Yeah," he said, firmer this time. "It's over."

"So what comes next?" Lopez asked.

Evan pulled back his shoulders. "I'm going back to the Amish. At least, I hope I am. If the bishop will let me."

Palmer pulled a stick of gum from his pocket, unwrapping it slowly. "That doesn't sound like a bad idea. A simpler life that's more peaceful."

"It's not all sunshine and daisies, but it's a good way to live. Safer, too."

"Then I hope it works out." Palmer popped the gum into his mouth, chewing thoughtfully.

Deputy Lopez tilted his head. "No reason to keep risking your life if you've got other things to live for."

Evan returned a curt nod. "I do, and I intend to. This job isn't where I belong anymore."

"Sometimes walking away from the stress

takes more strength than staying," Palmer said. "I can respect that."

The CSI van rolled into view. As it parked near the scene, the familiar thud of the sliding door echoed in the stillness. Two members of the crew emerged, clad in navy blue uniforms.

The CSI crew moved with an air of professionalism, their expressions serious as they began to catalog the evidence. The best thing to do was stay out of their way and let them work.

Pulling out his cell, Palmer dialed a number, his expression unreadable. "Go," he mouthed, waiting for the call to connect. "We'll regroup later and then make a statement to the press."

Evan scrubbed both hands over his face, then let them fall. "Sure. Whatever you say."

He turned and walked away, a silent weight settling across his shoulders. The loss of a human life left a bitter taste in his mouth. He couldn't help but wonder if there had ever been a moment when Lazzaro might have chosen differently? When someone could've reached him, pulled him back from the brink?

He shook his head. Apparently not.

Reaching his SUV, Evan's hand hovered over the handle. The dead man's image lingered in his mind. Somehow, it didn't feel like justice had been done. Lazzaro's death had all the markings of closure, but deep down, he knew better than to trust in appearances.

One shoe had dropped, but where was its partner? An injured man on the run couldn't possibly have managed alone. Someone had to be helping him.

Palmer wasn't having it. The ranger was itching to close the case, eager to mark it as a win for the good guys.

But a nagging doubt clung. Somewhere, a loose thread still dangled.

"Stop it," he muttered, trying to silence the unrest in his gut. The odds of finding an accomplice seemed bleak. If Lazarro had a cohort, he'd likely caught wind of the trouble, packed his bags and vanished.

Sliding behind the wheel, Evan rubbed the fatigue from his eyes. Since returning to duty, he'd powered through extra shifts. He'd tried to be out there, visible, ready and unafraid. If Lazarro had wanted another shot, he'd given him every opportunity to try. This time, Evan had been prepared to end it, once and for all, even if it meant crossing every line the Amish held dear.

Because of that, he'd come dangerously close to letting go of the things that really mattered. He'd allowed himself to start drifting again, convincing himself that catching the fugitive took precedence over attending Sunday services. Now, he realized how mistaken he'd been. Being away from *Gott* had been detrimental to his well-being in so many ways.

If your Bible isn't falling to pieces, your life usually is.

With quiet resolve, he lowered his head to pray. And to really mean what he said.

"I'm ready, Lord," he murmured. "Wherever You lead, I'll follow. Help me find my way back, to feel whole again and embrace the purpose You have set before me. Amen."

As he spoke, the heaviness began to lift, dissolving the burden he'd carried so long. It was a sensation he hadn't felt in years, a touch of grace that whispered of forgiveness.

Lifting his head, he wiped at the tears blurring his vision. The path ahead was filled with uncertainty, but he'd made a firm commitment to trust God's holy plan.

One he intended to keep.

Chapter Fifteen

The rest of the night was long, stretching endless hours.

Unable to rest, Isla sat in the living room. The soft ticking of the clock on the mantel was the only sound in the otherwise still house. Her body ached with exhaustion, but her spinning thoughts kept her wide awake.

Everything was gone. Every belonging, every memento, every piece of the life she'd built with Owen, all consumed by the merciless flames. The fire was swift and devastating, leaving behind nothing but ash and ruin.

She shivered despite the warmth of the fire dying in the hearth. Hazel had offered her and the children a place to stay, at least until she could figure out her next move. But she had no next move. Her life was in tatters.

How do I start over? With no money, no home and nothing but the clothes on their backs, how would she support Joel and Olivia? In the still of early morning, when all her worries were crashing down, she felt so very alone. So lost. She knew friends and neighbors would help, but it would still be hard. Her only means of earning a living had gone up in flames, but that didn't mean she wanted to be a charity case.

With a quiet sigh, she lowered her head, closing her eyes against the sting of tears. "Lord, I don't understand why this happened," she whispered, her voice barely audible. "But I know You have a plan, even if I can't see it right now. Please give me the strength to carry on. Show me the way forward and help me to trust that You will provide, just as You always have."

The prayer helped settled her nerves. She didn't have answers, not yet. But *Gott* would see them through, one step at a time.

Opening her eyes, she stared toward the window. The pale light of dawn had already crept past the horizon. The crunch of tires in the driveway shattered the stillness, followed by the sharp thud of a car door slamming shut.

Startled, Isla rose. She heard Evan's familiar steps on the porch just as the first streaks of sunlight spilled over the trees.

The front door creaked open.

Evan stepped inside, looking grim. His eyes were clouded with fatigue, and his face was drawn in tight lines. The faint scent of smoke still clung to his clothing, even though the fire had been hours ago. He rubbed a hand over his face, as if trying to wipe away the images of all the terrible things he'd witnessed that night.

"Is it true?" She couldn't bring herself to say that man's name, the man who had incinerated her world.

Evan hung his hat on the peg near the door. "Yeah. It's Sammy Lazzaro." Unholstering his gun, he placed it in a nearby cabinet, locking it with a soft click of the key.

"How…how did he die?"

"Looks like he took his own life," Evan said, rubbing the back of his neck. "But we won't know for sure until CSI has processed all the evidence."

Isla's breath caught. "What happens now?"

He shrugged, the gesture as empty as the outcome. "Case closed."

"Then it's really over?"

"Yeah," he said, his eyes shadowed with the exhaustion of the day. "I think so."

Isla's knees felt weak as the tension slowly drained from her body. The man who'd ripped her life apart, taken her peace, was gone. But with him went the one thing she'd clung to: hope for justice.

"*Danke* for telling me."

Evan gave a grim nod. "It's the best closure we're going to get in this case." Frustration flickered across his face. "Not how I wanted it to end, but at least it's over." He glanced at his watch. "I've got just enough time to wash up and grab some coffee before heading back to work. Palmer's handling the press release, and I need to be there."

"You haven't had a chance to rest," she said softly, concern in her voice.

"It doesn't matter," he said. "There's too much to get done."

"Let me fix you some breakfast before you head back."

Evan paused, a flicker of hesitation crossing his face. "I'd like that." He glanced at his hands, rubbing his fingers together absently. "I should probably wash up."

"Sounds *gut*."

Grateful for something to occupy her mind, Isla rose and hurried into the kitchen. She filled the percolator with fresh water and set it on the stove to perk while she prepared something for him to eat. The familiar rhythm of cooking grounded her frayed emotions amidst the chaos of her thoughts. As the aromas wafted through the air, she savored the fleeting sense of normalcy. For a moment, it felt as if the world hadn't completely turned upside down.

Evan appeared a few minutes later in a fresh shirt, he'd washed his face and combed down his hair. The tension that had shadowed him seemed to lighten just a little in the comforting space they shared.

"It's almost ready," she said, pouring a steaming cup of dark *kaffee*.

"Smells good," he said, gratefully accepting the cup she offered. Taking a sip, he looked around. "Where's Hazel?"

"She went to take her extra eggs to the neighbors."

"That's over a mile away," he said.

"She insists the fresh air does her *gut*," Isla explained. "Besides, Hambone needed the walk. She says he's getting too overweight. Stewart went, too."

Evan rolled his eyes. "Those three are quite the trio." He took another long drink. "Kids still in bed?"

"They were so tired I didn't want to wake them," she continued, transferring the crisp, golden bacon onto a stack of paper towels to drain. The eggs, whipped to a fluffy consistency with a pinch of salt, pepper and a splash of milk, waited to be poured into the frying pan.

"Understandable."

"I'm not sure how I'll explain everything to them when they do," she continued. "Most everything we've ever had is gone."

"I know it feels overwhelming right now. But we'll figure something out." Setting aside his cup, he stepped closer. "You're not alone in this. I'm going to be there. Every step of the way. You know that."

"I don't want to impose," she insisted.

"You're not imposing. You're family." He closed the space between them, his voice softening. "At least, I hope you will be one day."

"What are you saying?"

"I'm saying that I'm going to marry you one of these days."

Shock drizzled through her. "I... I thought you might have changed your mind."

His gazed locked on to hers. "Not for one single minute." He drew a steadying breath, gathering his resolve. "I'm ready to retire, and that's exactly what I'll be doing. After Palmer's done updating the press, I'll be putting in my resignation. Effective immediately."

"You mean it?"

"I do," he replied as he reached for her hand. "This isn't just about me anymore; it's about us. I want a future, with you. And I'm done letting anything stand in my way."

Isla's heart soared as his hands clasped hers. Then reality began to take root once more, fragile yet determined. "I wondered if you'd ever ask."

Evan gave a small nod, his voice low but certain. "As soon as I can make it happen, I will," he said, his voice firm yet soft. "Tonight opened my eyes to what truly matters. You and the kids are more important than this job. I almost lost you, and I won't make that mistake again."

"You're really serious?" she asked, blinking back tears.

"I am." Leaning forward, his lips brushed her forehead. "I love you. I always have."

Heart racing, Isla pulled back. With a shaky breath, she reached up to touch his cheek, her fingers brushing rough stubble. She could hardly believe how close he was, how real this moment felt.

"I—I love you, too." Before she could think it through, she stood on her tiptoes, reaching up to him.

It was as if time had paused, the world around them fading into a soft blur.

Evan's hands found her waist as his lips found hers.

Everything vanished: the worry, the pain and the lingering shadows of the past.

When they broke apart, Isla smiled.

Tenderness sparked in his eyes. "You're going to be my *fraa* someday," he said. "That's a promise."

Anticipation blossomed inside her. "Oh, *liebling*. I can't wait."

His smile faltered slightly as he glanced at his watch. "We'll talk later," he said. "I need to grab a bite and go."

"Of course." Returning to her cooking, she hurried to scramble the eggs. As she buttered the toast, she focused on the task, trying to steady her racing thoughts. Plating the food, she stole a glance at him. One day, he would be her *ehemann*, and she couldn't wait.

Before she could get the plate onto the table, a knock at the door interrupted.

Evan frowned. "Who could that be?"

"You sit down," Isla said, wiping her hands on a dishcloth. "I'll get it." Crossing into the living room, she opened the door.

Andrea Richards stood on the porch. Her blond hair was neatly pulled into a bun that framed her pert features. She carried a pristine white bakery box.

"Isla!" she exclaimed. "I heard about the fire. How very terrible for you. I hope you and the children are okay."

Isla blinked. It only made sense the news would have spread through town. Working at the sheriff's office, Andrea would have been among the first to know the details.

"*Danke*, we are," she said, stepping back. "Please, come in."

"I don't mean to interrupt, but I needed to see the sheriff."

"Of course." Isla motioned for her to follow. "This way, please."

Evan looked up as they entered the kitchen, his brow furrowing slightly. "Morning," he said, offering a slight smile. "Something up at the office?"

"Yeah, a few things," Andrea replied, her voice

steady, but there was an edge to it as she set the bakery box on the counter with a deliberate thud.

"I'm listening," he said, setting his cup aside.

Andrea's smile faded, her expression sharpening. "Good. Because I have a lot to say."

A chill slid down Isla's spine. Something was off—terribly, undeniably wrong. The warmth in the visitor's face had vanished, replaced by an intensity she'd never seen before. Andrea's eyes were no longer friendly, but calculating, intense. Predatory.

Breath evaporating, her instincts screamed at her to move. But her feet felt rooted, her mind struggling to catch up to the horror unfolding in front of her.

Reaching inside the pastry box, Andrea pulled out a gun.

The glint of metal in Andrea Richards' hand caught Evan's eye. A pistol. With a silencer.

He froze. No amateur here. She was a pro. "Andrea, what's going on?"

"Stay where you are." Her voice was as dangerous as the steel she held. "Don't make this harder than it has to be."

Evan's heart pounded. Trying to remain calm, he flicked a glance at Isla. Her face was pale, her eyes wide with fear.

His training kicked in. *Keep cool. Don't agitate.*

He spread his hands to show he was unarmed.

Easing closer to Isla, he knew he had to tread carefully. One wrong move could send everything spiraling into chaos. With an innocent woman and two sleeping children in the house, he couldn't afford to take any risks. The mere thought of Joel or Olivia waking up and wandering into this nightmare was terrifying. And Hazel… She could return home at any time.

"Just do what she says, and it'll be okay," he instructed Isla.

Isla slowly raised her hands, too. "Why are you doing this?"

Andrea smirked. "Because I've got unfinished business with the sheriff."

"Put the gun down," he said. "We can talk. Whatever you're trying to do, this isn't the way."

"Oh, I think this is exactly the way."

"Okay… Tell me what's on your mind."

"I'm just tying up a few loose ends for my brother," Andrea spat. "Now that Sammy's gone, someone's got to clean up the mess."

Shock buzzed through him. "Sammy Lazzaro is your brother?"

"Was," she snapped.

Evan's mind reeled. Andrea had always claimed to be an orphan with no family. When he'd hired her, she'd seemed like the perfect fit. Her references were solid, her record spotless, not even a single speeding ticket. Now, everything he thought he'd known about her was shattered.

"He was all I had, and you ruined him," she continued. "He couldn't walk, couldn't pull off jobs like he used to."

"You're Sammy's partner?"

"Yeah. Me." She laughed. "I was Sammy's eyes and ears, going where he couldn't."

Needing to keep her talking, Evan tried to draw out more information. "You scouted everything for the robberies?"

Their captor's expression twisted with pride. "I did. Once I picked the mark, Sammy did the rest." She gestured toward Isla. "The Amish are so easy to take advantage of. Look at her, keeping her money in a lockbox where anyone could see it."

Isla's eyes widened. "It was you all along."

Andrea snickered. "I paid you with your own money, and you were grateful to have it."

Isla gasped. "I trusted you, invited you into my home—"

"I can't help it if you're stupid," their captor sneered back. "Always so simpering and sweet. You make me sick."

Evan's chest tightened. Now he understood why the thief had always seemed one step ahead. As the department's secretary, Andrea had access to everything: schedules, patrol routes and other confidential information. She knew exactly where they would be and when, allowing Lazzaro to evade capture time and again.

"The Amish are innocent, hardworking people. Why would you want to take advantage of that?"

"Because it was easy." Andrea raised her weapon again. "Now I'm going to take everything from you. Just like you did to me."

"You don't have to do this," he said quietly. "There's still time to stop."

The gun in Andrea's hand wavered. "You don't understand. My brother always took care of me. He gave me everything our no-good parents never did. Money, clothes, a good education. He made sure I had all the nice things in life. He was my protector. And you ruined everything. Now he's gone, and I have nothing."

Evan's stomach twisted, replaying the Lazzaro death scene in his mind. "Did Sammy kill himself? Or was it you?"

Andrea's expression darkened. "I didn't see another way. After Sammy got hurt, he couldn't do much for me anymore. Letting him go felt like the kindest thing I could do. A mercy, even."

"Mercy?" he echoed. "Is that what you call it?"

"Sammy was suffering. His leg wasn't getting better. He wanted to turn himself in. But I couldn't let that happen."

"Because you were afraid he'd take you down with him?"

Andrea locked her gaze on his, unblinking, her resolve hardening. "I have a good life. Why let it go?" A shrug rolled off her shoulders. "Sammy had a problem, and I solved it." Her tone was almost pitying, as if she truly believed she'd done her sibling a favor.

"And I'm your next problem?"

Andrea didn't respond, just stared at him.

Suddenly, a mad giggle bubbled past her lips. "Not for much longer."

Evan tensed. Every nerve in his body was on high alert, his mind racing through options, strategies, anything that would give them a fighting chance.

"You don't have to do this," he said, thinking fast. "Put the gun down and we can figure this out."

The deranged woman violently rejected his plea. "You took everything I had," she snarled. "Now I'm taking yours." She gestured toward Isla.

"I'm the one you want," he grated. "Let Isla go. I'll go anywhere with you, no questions asked. Just don't hurt her."

"Please," Isla whispered, her voice steady yet filled with resolve. "My children...they've already lost so much."

Andrea refused to listen. Focus shifting again, her mouth twisted into a rictal grin.

"Did you enjoy the presents?"

Evan knew exactly what she meant. The wilting bouquet and cryptic note at Lila's grave, the unsettling birthday card, the toy coffin. Each was a sinister warning of what was to come. But the last act of cruelty—burning Isla's home—was the most chilling indication of her insanity.

"I get it, coming after me. But why Isla? Why drag her into this?"

"You love her," their captor sneered back, voice dripping with disdain. "The day you had her shawl, the look on your face said everything." Her expression faltered, flashing toward something almost human. Then, it vanished. "I'm going to destroy everything you love." She pointed the pistol directly at Isla. "Prepare to say goodbye."

Isla refused to cower. "I won't die in fear. *Gott* will protect us. If not in this world, then in the one to come."

With a cold smirk, Andrea stepped closer. "Guess you'll find out when you get there."

Evan moved instinctively, placing himself in front of Isla. "Please, don't hurt her." If a bullet was coming, it would meet him first.

"Don't," Isla whispered from behind. "If I am to face death, it will be without fear."

Andrea's lips curled as she leveled the gun. "How touching. But love stories don't always have happy endings." Her finger tightened on the trigger. "Time to say goodbye."

Evan tensed, waiting for the shot to ring out.

It never came.

Instead, a red rubber ball rolled across the kitchen floor, tapping against Andrea's shoe.

Andrea looked down, a flicker of puzzlement crossing her face. "What the—"

Stewart darted into the kitchen, his little paws scrabbling for the toy. Chattering with delight, he scrambled between her feet. Hambone lumbered in, snorting expectantly for a treat.

Startled, Andrea hopped back, waving the gun at the animals. "Go away! Shoo!"

Evan took advantage of her distraction. In a blur of motion, his hand shot out, seizing the skillet resting atop the stove. With all his strength, he swung it at Andrea's head. It connected with a thud.

"Oomph!" Gun slipping from her grasp, Andrea crumpled. She went down in a heap, unconscious before she even finished falling.

Breathing hard, Evan kicked the pistol out of her reach. "It's okay. I got her."

Isla gaped at the woman sprawled at her feet. "I think she's out cold."

His gaze flicked to his hand. He'd taken her down, all right. With a frying pan.

How am I supposed to explain this?

A raccoon, a pig and a piece of iron cookware. No one was going to believe him.

"I guess that settles it," he said, returning the pan to the stove.

A wry smile tugged Isla's lips. "*Ja*," she agreed. "It does."

Evan knelt, retrieving a pair of handcuffs from

his utility belt. With swift, practiced movements, he snapped the metal bracelets around Andrea's wrists with a firm click.

"Now this case is closed."

For the first time in weeks, he felt a burden lift from his shoulders. His duty done, he could walk away, head held high. He'd fulfilled his oath to those who'd trusted him to see justice served.

Hazel peeked around the edge of the doorframe. "Did we get her?"

"We did." He glanced at Andrea, a tangle of limbs and hair. No doubt a headache was in her future. As was a long stint behind bars.

"Call 911. Tell the dispatcher I've got Sammy Lazzaro's partner."

Hazel stepped into the kitchen. "I can't," she admitted, her expression sheepish. "I set my phone down for just a moment, and Stewart took it. I haven't been able to find it."

"It doesn't matter," Isla replied, wrapping her arms around Hazel in a grateful embrace. "You saved us and that's all that counts."

"While I was walking home, I had a terrible feeling something was wrong, like *Gott* was warning me." The old lady wrung her hands together, a hint of worry creasing her brow. "I couldn't think of anything else to do."

"I'll take care of it." Activating his tactical radio, Evan relayed details of the incident to the dispatcher. As he filled in the details, he glanced at the unusual duo. The raccoon had claimed his ball, batting it around with gleeful abandon. Hambone snorted, his beady eyes gleaming as he rooted around for the treat he was certain he deserved. The old yellow tom, who'd watched it all from the windowsill, blinked, unbothered by the entire mess.

Assured help was on the way, Evan ended the call. He reached down, giving the pig a scratch behind one pink ear. "Whatever you want, buddy, it's all yours."

Hambone responded with a delighted oink, nudging for more attention.

Evan patted the porker. "Don't get too excited."

Hazel's smile widened. "Guess he's worth having around."

"Thank the Lord, it's over." Isla's shoulders sagged with relief as she bowed her head. "I'll pray that poor woman gets the help she needs."

He reached for her hand, the gesture simple, but sure. "So will I."

Isla gave him a look. "Don't ever let go," she whispered, and her fingers tightened around his.

Evan's gaze stayed on her, this woman who had steadied his soul more times than he could name. She wasn't just his anchor; she was the reason he'd kept going. And if it came to it, he'd lay down his life for her without hesitation. Not out of duty. Out of love. A love he'd buried too long beneath denial.

"Never," he said.

And he meant it.

For the first time, he could see a life beyond the badge. It wasn't a dream, but something real. Solid. Within his reach.

But to claim it, he needed more than hope. He needed to find the strength to leave behind the man he had been and become the man he wanted to be.

For himself. For Isla. And for the family he hoped to have someday.

All he had to do was take the first step.

Epilogue

Three years later...

"See you next shift, Evan."

"*Ja*, you will," he said, stepping down from the van that had delivered him safely home after a hard night's work. The gentle light of dawn spilled over the property, casting a soft glow on the rambling old farmhouse.

As the driver turned the vehicle around and navigated back down the winding gravel lane, Evan paused, taking in the tranquil scene. The cool breath of morning, tinged with dew and distant woodsmoke, filled his lungs. Across the yard, he saw the illumination in the kitchen windows, a sign the inhabitants were up and around.

He smiled. It felt strange, thinking back on the long, twisting path that had brought him here. A path marked by mistakes, detours and second chances.

Many things had changed since he'd retired from law enforcement. After the grueling case with Sammy Lazzaro and his murderous partner, he'd known the time had come to put that life behind him. He'd put in his resignation, relieved but also uncertain about what lay ahead. For so long, the badge had been his identity.

Going back to school at his age had been scary, but the reward had been well worth the effort. Successfully completing his training as an EMT, he'd gone on to become licensed as a paramedic. Upon graduation, he'd taken a position with the fire department. His *Englisch* coworkers had been more than welcoming when he'd been hired. Over time, he'd earned their respect, not by flashy heroics but by his steady presence, his calm in the face of chaos.

Rejoining the church had been an important milestone, too. He'd wanted to be sure that his faith was truly his, not a weight he was obligated to carry. Thankfully, Bishop Harrison had worked with him, guiding him in his spiritual quest. By the end of his studies, he'd felt a deep conviction that his choice was right. He loved the Lord and yearned to serve.

The day of his baptism had been humbling and profound. With his parents and brothers at his side, the rest of the community had surrounded him with support. He'd stood with bowed head as the bishop prayed over him, then felt the cool touch of water marking his commitment to a life of simplicity and devotion.

It wasn't long after that he'd gone to Isla, nervously clasping her hands as he formally asked her to be his wife.

She'd said yes.

After that, there was no turning back.

As he neared the door, Evan looked at the garden. He and Joel had been working together to till the soil for Isla's herb patch. Joel had done most of the labor, taking on his role with a seriousness beyond his years. Growing taller and stronger, Joel rarely suffered from the asthma that had plagued him when he was younger.

Proud of the youngster's efforts, he continued up onto the porch. Just as he reached the front door, it swung open.

Face glowing with the radiance of impending motherhood, Isla leaned against the frame. Her hand rested on her large, round belly.

"I thought I heard the van pull up." Her eyes sparkled, but there was exhaustion, too. Creating a haven of comfort, she'd worked hard to add her own touches to Hazel's old *haus*. Rather than build a new place, they'd opted to remain with his aunt. Renovations were slow, but steady. They'd already knocked down several walls upstairs, turning two rooms into one to create a spacious new nursery.

"We had a call right before end of shift," he said, explaining his late arrival. "Car accident."

"Was anyone hurt?"

"Thankfully it was minor." Once again, a careless *Englisch* driver had rear-ended a buggy. "No one was injured." The driver, however, had received a ticket, written up by none other than the new sheriff. After he'd stepped down, Diego Lopez had thrown his hat into the ring. Running a solid campaign, the deputy was elected in a landslide.

"I'm always worried when you're late getting off."

Evan sighed, the pressure of her concern settling on his shoulders. Normally, he worked a grueling schedule: twenty-four hours on, then twenty-four off, rotating through three shifts, followed by four solid days of rest. But lately, the unpredictability of his hours gnawed at him, amplifying his anxiety. With the baby overdue, he worried about leaving for any long stretch of time.

"I'm fine," he assured her. "The ones who deserve the concern right now are you and this little one." He reached out, resting his palm flat against her belly. "I'll breathe easier when the *boppli* makes an appearance."

Isla laughed. "It's only a week past the date," she said, placing her hand over his. "The *kind* will come when it's time."

He grinned. "I can't wait."

"Me, either."

Sharing a quick kiss, they laughed softly.

"Come on," she said, nudging him toward the kitchen. "The *kaffee* is hot, and breakfast is almost ready. I hope you're hungry."

"Starved."

Hanging his backpack by the front door, Evan peeled off his jacket, then ran his fingers through his thick beard. Neatly trimmed, it wasn't a distraction, pairing well with the clothes he wore for work. Accompanied by khaki pants, his white shirt was emblazoned with the department's patches, his name and rank.

A sense of pride swelled in him; wearing the uniform symbolized more than just his role in the community. It represented a bridge between his Amish roots and a commitment to serve. He knew he was paving the way for others in the Plain community, too. Five other Amish men had stepped up to volunteer, giving him a sense of camaraderie and purpose like never before.

As he stepped into the kitchen, the aroma of freshly brewed *kaffee* enveloped him, mingling with the scent of sizzling bacon and warm cinnamon rolls.

Breakfast was being served, but so were other surprises. Namely, a whole bunch of baby skunks.

Taking over most of the kitchen floor, Joel and Olivia were attempting to settle the trio down. Wriggling and squeaking, the little black-and-white critters tumbled over one another as they attempted to climb out of the basket. Hazel hovered nearby, her gaze sharp and watchful, ready to step in if things got out of hand.

Evan steered clear. "I thought you said you were retiring from rescue."

Now a spry eighty, the old lady waggled a finger. "These little ones needed help, and I couldn't say no. Their mother was hit by a car last night." She gestured to the basket. "We'll be taking care of them until they're old enough to be released."

Olivia backed her up. "*Tante* Hazel is teaching me how to become a rehabber. We have bottles and some kitten milk replacement to feed them."

Isla laughed. "They're not so bad. And look at them. They need love just like any other creature."

Before he could respond, Hambone trotted into the kitchen. Right behind him came Stewart, shuffling in with his usual sly curiosity. Both animals snuffled curiously around the basket. Hambone's tail wagged with enthusiasm as he nudged one of the kits. The little animal squeaked in surprise and wobbled backward.

"Hambone, be nice!" Joel warned, laughing. "You'll scare them."

Hazel chuckled, undeterred. "Let him be. Hambone's just saying hello. He knows what it's like to be the newcomer."

As he watched Olivia and Joel fuss over the skunks, a warm feeling settled in. This was what home felt like.

He allowed a few minutes to revel in the delightful absurdity of the morning. As always, the house was full of a variety of animals. Inspired by Hazel's work with wildlife, Olivia had taken a keen interest in animal welfare and rescue. Choosing to continue her education beyond the eighth grade, she hoped to go on to college and study to be a vet tech.

Joel had chosen to follow in his father's footsteps and become a cobbler. He presently worked part-time as an apprentice to carry on the trade Owen had begun teaching him before he passed.

The scene filled Evan with warmth, a delightful blend of chaos and compassion. It was also a vivid reminder of the life he and Isla were building together. Although he could never replace the children's father, both *kinder* had embraced him, eagerly anticipating the arrival of their new sibling.

Stepping around them, he headed to the stove. "Just remember, I'm not the one taking care of the stinkers," he warned. "You two are on your own if they turn out to be little terrors."

Isla's laughter rang out. "That's what you said about the kittens Olivia's cat had. And we both know how that turned out."

Sipping his drink, Evan's gaze drifted toward the sunlit windowsill, where a familiar scene unfolded. Perched on the windowsill, Hazel's old yellow tom supervised a trio of cute calicos, playfully batting at Stewart's red ball. Mama cat Mittens sat nearby, proud of her little brood.

"*Ja*," he murmured. "I guess we do."

A surge of gratitude filled him. Each day he

was reminded of the wonderful chaos that came with family life; each laugh, each struggle and each moment of tenderness woven into the fabric that made a house a home.

The Lord has truly blessed me.

And he wouldn't have it any other way.

Walking away from the shadows of his past, he'd finally found the path he was meant to follow. His wife and children were his anchors now, the unwavering light that reminded him what truly mattered: serving the Lord, resilience and shared dreams.

Together, they would face whatever tomorrow might bring, secure in the knowledge that *Gott*'s grace would envelop and protect them.

For the rest of their lives.

* * * * *

*If you liked this story
from Pamela Desmond Wright,
check out her previous Love Inspired books:*

Her Amish Refuge
Her Surprise Amish Match
Bonding over the Amish Baby
The Cowboy's Amish Haven

*Available now from Love Inspired!
Find more great reads at
www.LoveInspired.com.*

Dear Reader,

I can't tell you how much joy it brought me to write An Amish Widow's Hope. This book has been a labor of love, and I'm so thrilled to share it with you.

From the moment Evan stepped back into Isla's life, I knew their journey would be something special. Their past as childhood sweethearts, torn apart by his choice to leave the Amish community, set the stage for a second-chance romance that tugged at my heartstrings. Evan's struggle to find his way back to God after years of doubt, and Isla's unwavering belief that sustained her through loss and danger, reminded me of the power of grace and trust. Their journey isn't just about love for each other—it's about finding peace in something greater.

For those new to the *Texas Amish Brides* series, this is the fifth book. To explore the entire collection and stay updated on new releases, visit www.pameladesmondwright.com. You'll find all the details, along with exciting news on what's coming next!

I love hearing from my readers, so feel free to send me a note! If email isn't your thing, I can be reached at PO Box 165, Texico, NM, 88135-0165.

Thank you all for coming on this journey with me. I'll be back soon with more love, more faith and plenty of new Amish adventures!

Blessings always,
Pamela Desmond Wright

Get up to 4 Free Books!

**We'll send you 2 free books from each series you try
PLUS a free Mystery Gift.**

FREE
Value Over
$25

Both the **Love Inspired**® and **Love Inspired**® **Suspense** series feature compelling
novels filled with inspirational romance, faith, forgiveness and hope.

YES! Please send me 2 FREE novels from the Love Inspired or Love Inspired Suspense series
and my FREE gift (gift is worth about $10 retail). After receiving them, if I don't wish to receive
any more books, I can return the shipping statement marked "cancel." If I don't cancel, I will
receive 6 brand-new Love Inspired Larger-Print books or Love Inspired Suspense Larger-
Print books every month and be billed just $7.19 each in the U.S. or $7.99 each in Canada.
That is a savings of 20% off the cover price. It's quite a bargain! Shipping and handling is
just 50¢ per book in the U.S. and $1.25 per book in Canada.* I understand that accepting
the 2 free books and gift places me under no obligation to buy anything. I can always return
a shipment and cancel at any time by calling the number below. The free books and gift are
mine to keep no matter what I decide.

Choose one: ☐ **Love Inspired**   ☐ **Love Inspired**   ☐ **Or Try Both!**
              Larger-Print   **Suspense**   (122/322 & 107/307 BPA G36Z)
              (122/322 BPA G36Y)   **Larger-Print**
                                           (107/307 BPA G36Y)

Name (please print)

Address   Apt. #

City   State/Province   Zip/Postal Code

Email: Please check this box ☐ if you would like to receive newsletters and promotional emails from Harlequin Enterprises ULC and its affiliates.
You can unsubscribe anytime.

Mail to the **Harlequin Reader Service:**
IN U.S.A.: P.O. Box 1341, Buffalo, NY 14240-8531
IN CANADA: P.O. Box 603, Fort Erie, Ontario L2A 5X3

Want to explore our other series or interested in ebooks? Visit www.ReaderService.com or call 1-800-873-8635.

LIRLIS25